THE
SLEEPING
LADY

THE SLEEPING LADY

a mystery

Bonnie C. Monte

She Writes Press, a BookSparks imprint
A Division of SparkPointStudio, LLC.

Published 2018

Printed in the United States of America

ISBN: 978-1-63152-387-8 pbk
ISBN: 978-1-63152-388-5 ebk
Library of Congress Control Number: 2018931553

For information, address:
She Writes Press
1563 Solano Ave #546
Berkeley, CA 94707

She Writes Press is a division of SparkPoint Studio, LLC.

To Hillary and Emma,
who inspire me every day.

CHAPTER 1

Yoga wasn't helping. Despite forty-five minutes of stretches, contortions, and deep breathing, I was still in a foul mood. "Focus on the breath," the lithe young instructor urged the class as I sat cross-legged on my mat. Eyes closed, I tried to force my mind back to the slow, rhythmic inhalations and exhalations, but resentment was my mantra at that moment. Why had Thalia insisted on jetting off to Paris during our busiest season, leaving me to run the shop on my own? She could have easily negotiated the purchase of those quilts by email. More to the point, why had I agreed to let her go? Maybe Peter was right. I was a pushover when it came to my business partner.

"As you inhale, feel yourself filling up with light," intoned the teacher. "Now exhale, and release all negativity." Damn it. Because of Thalia's last-minute jaunt, this was the eighth straight day that I would be in the shop. And I still wasn't keeping up with everything. There were bills to be paid; there was merchandise to be ordered. And I suddenly remembered that a big estate sale that sounded promising was happening today up in Healdsburg. I'd have to miss it.

"Shit!" I said, my frustration reaching critical mass. Oops. Had I actually said that out loud? I opened my eyes to find surprised faces turned in my direction. The instructor, though, seemed unfazed. "Stay focused on the breath," she serenely reminded the class, making her way toward the back of the studio where I sat. As she leaned over me, I tried to look meditative. "Everything OK?" she asked softly.

"Sorry about that," I murmured, chagrined. Swearing in yoga class was no doubt a black mark on my karma, meted out by whatever higher power was keeping score. "I'm fine. Just a cramp in my leg," I said to the instructor. Lying, too. Another demerit. The teacher nodded, then returned to the front of the room.

I managed to make it through the rest of the class with no further outbursts. But as we were lying prone in our final meditation, my phone, stuffed in my purse in one of the wall cubbies, began to ring. Another faux pas! I'd forgotten to silence it. After what seemed like an eternity but was actually only four rings, it stopped. My cheeks burned, but at least no one knew I was the offender. The minute class ended, I grabbed my stuff and beat a hasty retreat.

Stepping outside into the sunshine, I shook my shoulder-length dark hair free of its elastic band and inhaled the scent of roasting coffee beans wafting into the street from the corner café. Although the temperature would probably reach the high nineties by the afternoon, right now the early morning weather was absolutely perfect. I checked my phone. A missed call from Thalia. Not surprisingly, there was no message. Whenever I didn't answer right away Thalia typically hung up—yet another of her annoying habits. "Why should I leave a message?" she'd said when I complained. "You always call back without listening to the message first and I have to say everything all over again." She had a point. I was in no mood to talk to her. I'd call her later.

It was a short walk from Fairfax's bustling little downtown to my house on tree-lined Hickory Street. "I'm back," I announced as I opened the front door and walked down the hall. Peter was sitting at the pine table in the high-ceilinged kitchen, sipping black coffee and reading the morning news on his tablet. Jasper lay at his feet in a puddle of sunlight. The pudgy yellow lab thumped his tail in greeting but stayed where he was, keeping his eyes focused on the bagel that Peter was lifting to his mouth. I smiled at the sight of them. Peter was definitely a creature of habit, starting every morning sitting in the same chair, drinking coffee from the same mug.

True, sometimes his adherence to order and routine was a bit much. For instance, his thing about how to fold the towels in the linen closet made me roll my eyes, although I complied just to shut him up. After all, it had been his house long before I'd moved in five years ago, and if he liked his towels folded in thirds, I could handle that. Maybe it was his fanatical attention to detail that made him such a successful architect and builder.

"Have you been feeding the dog your bagel?" I asked with suspicion.

"Nope."

Not true, I was sure. I opened the fridge and poured myself a glass of orange juice. "So I swore in yoga class," I announced between swallows. "And then I lied."

Peter laughed. "Come here," he said, pulling me onto his lap. "You may not be the perfect student, but you look great in the pants," he said, patting my Lycra-clad bottom. OK, maybe yoga did have its advantages. He began kissing my neck. "Want to go back upstairs?"

"Mmm. But I can't. I have to get to the shop."

"What about the fair Thalia?" Peter asked, releasing his embrace. "How come you're the one who does all the work—"

"She's on a buying trip," I said quickly, cutting him off. "Some last-minute thing. It's no big deal." I didn't need him to start one of his rants about Thalia: how she was spoiled and inconsiderate, how she took advantage of me, blah, blah, blah. "Besides, I thought you were meeting with a client this morning."

"I am, but not for a few hours," Peter said, stroking my back. "And they've already seen preliminary drawings, so this meeting is just to sign the contract. We'll have no trouble getting it approved. I'm making the space a lot more usable, but I'm hardly increasing the footprint of the house. Even the town tree-huggers will be happy with it."

Fairfax, our little town twenty miles north of San Francisco, was decidedly anti-development. The locals—an amiable assortment of hippies, yuppies, and everything in between—were not eager for change. And I was of a similar mind, although Peter and I sometimes locked horns over it. As the San Francisco Bay Area sprawled ever onward, Fairfax, nestled at the foot of Mount Tamalpais, remained an oasis of green.

"I need to shower and get out of here," I said, extricating myself from Peter's embrace and heading upstairs. Climbing back into bed with my husband was certainly tempting, but I had to get going.

By the time I came back down to the kitchen, Peter was on his cell phone immersed in business. I gave him a quick kiss, threw some fruit and a yogurt into my bag, and grabbed the dog's leash from its hook by the front door. "Come on Jasper, let's go."

The tall butterfly bush next to the porch steps was in full bloom, and I leaned into it to inhale its fragrance while Jasper found a spot to pee in. The front yard, now at its midsummer peak, was a happy mélange of colors and shapes, more suited perhaps to a cottage in the Cotswolds than a 1920s craftsman bungalow, as Peter liked to point out. If he had his way, it would be all geometric beds, with perfectly manicured boxwood. But while I might humor him on towel-folding, one area where I refused to budge was the garden. Growing up in a Brooklyn apartment, I'd long coveted a garden of my own. Now that I had one, I wasn't about to forgo my shrub roses and lilacs. I led Jasper through the gate to the Volvo parked out front.

It was only an eight-minute drive from our house in Fairfax to Le Jardin, the shop Thalia and I ran in the quaint neighboring town of San Anselmo. The small store, sandwiched between two pricey antique shops, sold home and garden decor, some new, some vintage, most of it from France. The economic downturn appeared to have had no impact in Marin County, where people willingly paid high prices for the perfect treasure.

I unlocked the door, turned on the lights, and started a pot of coffee in the small back room that served as both office and supply room. While it was brewing, I checked the phone messages, then opened the back door to let Jasper out. The tiny shop had a correspondingly tiny concrete patio out back, but I had spruced it up with dozens of containers overflowing with flowers and herbs. Chairs, obelisks, and other merchandise were sprinkled among them, creating a setting that invited customers to sit and linger on warm days. Morning glories climbed a trellis in a wide metal planter that was previously a Victorian laundry tub. I gave all the plants a drenching, then filled Jasper's water bowl, snipped a few sweet pea stems, and put them in an antique mustard jar on the counter. At ten o'clock, I turned the hand-lettered sign from "closed" to "open."

A steady stream of customers kept me and my part-time employee Susan busy all morning. Well, I told myself as I turned to help another customer, being too busy was preferable to the alternative. Still, I was thankful that Thalia was flying home tonight. I was wrapping up a galvanized French flower bucket for a young couple when my friend Sonia came in.

"Hi, Rae." She greeted me with a hug. "I just got a call for a photo shoot tomorrow. Can I borrow a few props?"

"Of course, help yourself."

Sonia worked as a prop stylist, setting up locations for magazine and catalog photo shoots. She was known for her airy, pared-down interiors, which amused me because her own funky cottage was an eclectic hodgepodge. She lived high up in the hills of Fairfax, along with two dogs, numerous cats, and a goat. I was pretty sure she let the goat in the house when no one was looking. Sonia's wardrobe blended multiple decades, usually worn all at once. Today she sported a long flouncy skirt with a beaded vintage sweater, hiking boots, and clip-on rhinestone earrings. She scooped up a few antique kitchen canisters and an enamel sign from an old tobacco shop. "This stuff is perfect," she said. "Can I borrow it until Tuesday?"

"Sure."

"Hi Jasper, you lump." Sonia stooped down to scratch the dog behind the ears. "So how's Thalia?" she asked me.

"Fine. She's flying back tonight."

"Hey, didn't she do the last two buying trips? I thought *you* were supposed to go to France next month."

"That was the plan, but she had some friend she really wanted to see over there . . ." I waved my hand dismissively.

"'Friend,' huh? Is he young and tasty?"

"Oh, come on. She's very happy with Garrett."

"Why wouldn't she be? The guy's a successful attorney and they live in a ten-room house in Ross. But that doesn't mean she can't have a lover in Paris."

I dismissed Sonia's theory with a laugh, although it was true that Thalia had been extremely vague about why she, rather than me, needed to go to Paris so urgently.

"Let's have dinner with her when she's back and we'll worm it out of her," Sonia suggested. "Since my own sex life is nonexistent right now, I can at least hear about hers. How about next Tuesday?"

"Sounds good. I'll check with her."

"OK. Bye, sweetie."

Susan and I had our hands full until shortly after noon. Finally there was a lull, and Susan stepped out to grab some lunch for the two of us. I was tidying the shelves when the shop phone rang. Thalia's familiar husky voice had a tense edge. "Rae, it's me. I'm on a layover at JFK. My flight gets in around six this evening. Let's have a drink afterward."

"Um, sure. Want to come over?"

"No, no, let's go out. I need to talk to you. I'll phone you on my way home from the airport."

"OK. How did the buying go? Did you get a good deal on the quilts?"

"Quilts?" She sounded distracted. I heard her take a long drag on a cigarette.

"Is anything wrong?" I asked.

"No . . ." Thalia paused. "Actually, yes. I'll tell you when I see you."

That evening I strolled the ten blocks from my house to Fairfax's local brew pub, enjoying the balmy weather. I gazed up at Mount Tam, which towered above the leafy streets, and marveled at how lucky I was to live in this slice of paradise.

I was sipping a Lagunitas pale ale at a back table when Thalia walked in. Heads turned: the men's because she had honey-blond hair and legs a mile long, the women's because her cashmere sweater, silk skirt, and custom-made Italian boots deserved a second look. I was used to Thalia commanding all the attention. It's not that I thought I was unattractive. But at five foot three with a mane of curly dark hair, being next to pale, willowy Thalia sometimes made me feel like a swarthy dwarf.

Thalia ordered a martini and frowned when the server told her that the only alcohol available was beer. "Fine, I'll have a mineral water with lime," she said with impatience, and then she turned her attention back to me. "Look at this." She took a folded piece of paper out of her purse and passed it across the table. I read the typed words: *I know about your affair. Prepare to pay.*

"What's this?"

"It was left at my hotel yesterday morning in an envelope." Her mineral water arrived, and she took several sips as I looked at the note again. She set the glass down and brushed her hair back off her forehead. I saw fine lines around her gray eyes, lines that I'd never noticed before. I sat in silence waiting for further explanation. None came.

"So just who does this person think you're having an affair with?" I asked.

"Etienne."

"Who the hell is Etienne?" Why couldn't Thalia simply get to the point, without making me interrogate her?

"I met him at the beginning of last year. We've been together the past three times I was in France."

"You mean you're cheating on Garrett?" I asked accusingly.

Thalia gave me an amused smile. "Sweetie, wake up and smell the roses. It's not unheard of to have an affair."

"Coffee," I said sharply.

"What?"

"Coffee. It's 'Wake up and smell the coffee,' 'Stop and smell the roses,'" I snapped. "You're mixing metaphors."

"You're angry at me," Thalia said, stating the obvious. "I know I should have told you about him a long time ago." She reached into her leather bag and pulled out a charcoal-gray box. "I brought you a present."

I recognized the box instantly—it was from Ladurée, and no doubt filled with the patisserie's irresistible macarons. Thalia was still talking. "He's marvelous. You'll understand when you meet him."

"And when would that be?" I said coldly, nowhere near ready to forgive Thalia for withholding such a bombshell, pastries notwithstanding.

"At Garrett's birthday party in a few weeks. Etienne is coming to San Francisco with his wife and son. They're—"

"Wife?" I interrupted, raising my eyebrows.

"Yes, Renata."

I made my voice as icy as possible. "It wasn't her name I was asking about."

"All right, all right, yes, he's married. I can't help that, can I?"

"No, but presumably you could help screwing him." I opened the box and broke off half a rose-petal macaron. Heavenly. Mouth full, I glared at Thalia, who sat in silence, looking utterly serene. Finally my curiosity got the better of me. "OK," I sighed. "Tell me."

"We met at the flea market. We both had our eye on the same candelabra, and he very gallantly allowed me to have it. We ended up walking all over town together. We had dinner. And, well, what can I say? There was an instant connection." There often was. Although many men found Thalia too frosty and intimidating, I remembered from our college days that those who were attracted to her fell in love in about five minutes.

"Is it serious?" I asked.

"Yes." Thalia's face took on a dreamy expression that I found disconcerting—this was an entirely new side of my levelheaded business partner.

"So what about Garrett? Are you going to leave him?"

"God, no," Thalia said quickly. "At least not now." She paused. "Of course, we've talked about it. Etienne and I. But we're not ready. Renata could make things difficult."

No kidding, I thought, since you're stealing her husband. "So what's the deal with the note?" I asked.

"Oh, I have some ideas about that. There's someone who works with Etienne—Marcel. He doesn't like my being around. That's because I caught him going through Etienne's papers and I confronted him. Poor Etienne is so trusting." The dreamy look returned, but I nipped that in the bud.

"How would he know which hotel to leave the note at?" I asked. "Do you think he followed you?"

"Maybe. But he could easily have heard Etienne mention it."

"So he's threatening to reveal the affair to . . . what's her name, Renata," I prompted.

"I guess. But I'm not too concerned about that." She took a sip of her water. "After all, it's France. It's not unusual to have a lover. I'm more worried about Garrett finding out. It could get really ugly. He's about to be made partner in his law firm. The other two partners are devoted family men. One even leads a youth ministry group. Garrett can't have any sordid secrets."

"It's not really Garrett's sordid secret," I pointed out. "It's yours." Nor was I convinced that Etienne's wife would be so open-minded about her husband's extramarital romance. "Do you think Renata knows?"

Thalia shrugged. "Perhaps. She did insist on coming along on this trip. She told Etienne that she wanted their son to see San Francisco, but maybe she just wants to keep an eye on him." She thought about that for a few seconds, then shook her head. "No, I doubt she knows. She works in her father's diamond importing business, and she's always on some business trip or another."

"Maybe she's having an affair too."

"It's certainly possible."

"So how old is Candelabra Man?" I asked.

"Three years older than us. He's thirty-nine. He runs an import-export company in Paris."

I sat in silence, my anger rising at Thalia's laissez-faire attitude. Did her marriage mean nothing to her? Fleetingly, I wondered if Peter shared this breezy view of adultery. The thought of him being unfaithful made me queasy. I ate the other half of my macaron. "How come you never told me about this affair?" I demanded.

"I thought you'd disapprove."

"Thalia, I'm no prude," I said, offended.

She smiled. "Well you do disapprove, don't you?"

Her logic was irrefutable. "I . . . I was just shocked. Momentarily." I reached for another macaron.

CHAPTER 2

"We don't have to stay long at this thing, do we?" Peter asked as we drove down Sir Francis Drake Boulevard on our way to Ross. Tonight was the party Thalia was throwing in honor of Garrett's fortieth birthday and his promotion to partner at the law firm. And, as promised, she'd invited Etienne and his family, who were in town. Well, I reflected, she certainly liked to live on the edge. I was probably more worried than she was about Garrett noticing what was up.

"Come on, you always have a good time at their parties," I said.

"I'm not in a partying mood, I guess."

"What's wrong?" I asked. "Is it Arizona again?" Peter had been buying rental property in Phoenix, having decided it was the key to a prosperous retirement. But it seemed like every day there was some new headache with a problem tenant or a building repair. Tonight he'd been on the phone for nearly an hour before we got in the car, and the conversation didn't sound cordial.

"Don't start with me about Arizona," he said sharply. "You think I want to end up broke like my father? He left my mother with nothing when he died. I will *not* do that to my family." He scowled at me.

"Relax. Nobody's dying anytime soon." I knew that the difficult finances during his childhood had left their mark on Peter. Even though we were comfortably off thanks to his thriving design-build contracting business, he never stopped worrying about money. And, I had to admit, I wasn't helping much. The shop was thriving, but running a store was an expensive proposition, especially with all our buying trips abroad. Thalia and I each drew a meager salary.

"Well, we have to at least stay until they sing 'Happy Birthday.' Besides," I added, "you might find tonight more interesting than you were expecting."

"Oh?"

"Peter, Thalia has a lover."

"Seriously?"

"And he's going to be there tonight."

"Are you telling me that one of Garrett's friends is sleeping with Thalia? My God."

We turned off the main road onto the wooded lanes of Ross, with their impressive mansions set well back from the street. "No, nothing like that. This is a man she met in France. He's in town with his family, so they're coming tonight too. And guess what else," I said excitedly. "She got a blackmail note!" As soon as I said it, I felt a twinge of guilt for sharing Thalia's secret. But Peter's look of surprise was so gratifying that I went on to recount the whole story, ending with Thalia's suspicion of someone named Marcel.

Peter was silent for a moment, then said, "That's not really blackmail, you know. It's just an anonymous note. Still . . ."

"I know!" I said. "It's creepy, isn't it?"

Their house came into view. Peter steered the car up the long, circular drive and handed the keys to one of the two young parking valets who had been hired for the night. Thalia and Garrett certainly didn't skimp when they threw a party.

We made our way up the grand front stairs and entered the high-ceilinged foyer, where a marble table bore a huge arrangement of fragrant peonies. Swept up in their heady scent, with the strains of classical music drifting in from the living room and the crush of elegantly clad guests propelling us forward, I half expected to be welcomed by Jay Gatsby himself, cigar in hand.

Instead, it was Garrett who greeted us as we stepped into the living room. He clapped Peter on the back and shook his hand vigorously, then squeezed me in a too-tight bear hug. Garrett was a large man, over six feet tall, and beefy. Not fat—at least not yet—but substantial, his face already showing a hint of jowls and his pale blond hair streaked with gray. Tonight his normally ruddy face was even redder than usual. It was evident that he'd already had a few drinks. "Rae, you look great. Are you feeling better?" I nodded, puzzled. "Come, I have a friend I want you to meet," Garrett said to Peter. "He's in the market for a brilliant architect. Rae, go find yourself a drink."

I worked my way over to the bar, where I requested a glass of red wine. Uniformed servers moved smoothly through the crowd bearing trays of hors d'oeuvres. I made small talk with various guests as I scanned the scene for Thalia. "Such a marvelous room," a stiffly coiffed elderly woman was saying. "I must find out who her decorator is." I murmured something neutral. Thalia, of course, had done the decor herself, but I wasn't sure how well that information would be received by this snobby guest. The setting really was lovely. The chandelier cast its soft light on the golden yellow walls and silk draperies, setting the room aglow. Many of the furnishings were family heirlooms— the Oriental carpets that graced the gleaming hardwood floors, the oil paintings of various relatives, the ornately carved walnut credenza. But Thalia had kept it from being predictable or stodgy by deftly mixing in modern pieces, as well as artwork from some of her favorite painters. The overall effect was comfortable and luxurious.

Just then Thalia appeared at my side, looking luminous in a shimmery copper-colored dress that left her shoulders bare. Her normally pale face was flushed with excitement. She steered me toward a small group standing by the piano and made introductions. "Rae, this is Etienne Duchamp, his wife Renata, and their son, Julien. My business partner, Rae Sullivan." Renata smiled and nodded. Etienne shook my hand. "Delighted to meet you," he said with a thick accent.

Everything about Etienne suggested restraint, from his lean physique to his closely cropped dark hair to his impeccably tailored suit. He and Renata made an odd couple. She was a good six inches shorter than her husband and blonde—bleached as far as I could tell. She could have been quite pretty, but her heavy makeup was horribly unflattering, giving her face a mask-like appearance. A large diamond graced her ring finger, with more diamonds encircling her throat.

We chatted about Etienne's company and the business meetings he had scheduled in the Bay Area. "I'm going to bring him by to visit the store," Thalia said, touching his arm lightly. A palpable undercurrent of electricity passed between them. Surely his wife must have sensed that something was afoot. But no. She seemed unconcerned.

"Is this your first visit to San Francisco, Renata?" I asked as Thalia drifted off to another cluster of guests.

"Oh, no. I have been coming here for years. But this is Julien's first trip"—she put a hand on her son's shoulder—"and my first visit to Marin County." She pronounced it "marine." "It is very beautiful."

Julien looked like a younger version of his dad. I guessed him to be sixteen or seventeen. We struck up a conversation—he spoke English quite well—and he confided that he was writing a screenplay. He lowered his voice. "I'm basing the villain on my father's assistant, Marcel."

"Really? Why is that?"

"Because he snoops in the office when my father isn't watching him. And he pretends to be so nice to Thalia—I mean, Mrs. Holcombe—but I hear what he calls her when she's not in the room."

Before I could pursue this intriguing line of conversation, two more guests joined our little circle. A pleasant man with sandy hair and steel-rimmed glasses was introduced as Etienne's office manager, Jerome. "And this is Marcel, my assistant," Etienne said.

"*Enchanté*," said Marcel with a slight bow. With his bulbous eyes and sallow skin, he reminded me of a frog. His homeliness was even more pronounced in its contrast with his stocky, well-muscled build that was evident beneath his suit jacket.

"So you are the partner of Madame Holcombe," Marcel remarked. "I have heard a great deal about you." His stare made me uncomfortable. We struggled through several minutes of stilted conversation, until I spotted Sonia across the room and waved to her.

"You're looking rather fabulous," I said as she approached. Jerome and Marcel seemed to agree by the way their eyes were riveted on Sonia. Her skin-tight emerald-green dress showed every curve, and her forties hairdo was a perfect match. Plus she'd dyed her tresses a flaming orange for the occasion. I made the introductions. Renata was clearly uncomfortable in Sonia's presence, barely acknowledging her. Then, claiming to be hot, she insisted her son and husband accompany her out to the garden.

As they left Sonia said, "I'm dying for a drink. Where's the bar?"

"Allow me," Jerome said gallantly. "What would you like?"

"I'll come with you," Sonia said, linking her arm through his. They made their way toward the dining room, leaving me with Marcel. More small talk followed, until I finally excused myself and turned to leave, bumping into the man behind me.

"Why, it's little Rae," he said with delight.

"Luc!" I embraced him. Thalia's half brother bore a resemblance to her, with the same gray eyes and angular jaw. But he had none of Thalia's frailty. His shoulders were broad, and where she was fair, his hair was dark. We had met in France years ago when Thalia and I were spending our junior year of college abroad. Funny how Luc had seemed so much older than us then—a man of the world, who took us to bohemian parties and taught me to eat snails without flinching. Looking at him now, though, in his tweed jacket and starched black shirt, I realized with surprise that he was only a few years older than me, probably about the same age as Peter.

"How are you?" I asked, squeezing his hand.

"I'm well." When he smiled, his eyes crinkled in his tan face. "And you! You look wonderful." The last time he'd seen me, I'd been a chubby nineteen-year-old with frizzy hair.

"So do you," I said. "You haven't changed a bit. Are you still living in Paris?"

"No, I'm in the countryside now," he said. "I have a little farm."

"Farm!" I exclaimed. The notion of a life spent working the

land was my idea of nirvana. Of course, not the getting up early part. Or the backbreaking labor part. "What do you grow?"

"Oh, a little bit of everything. I have some chickens, too, for the eggs. And there are my girls, Jolie, Belle, and Madeleine."

I stole a glance at his left hand. No ring. "Your daughters?" I asked.

He laughed heartily as Thalia came up behind us. "They're his potbellied pigs," she said. "He spoils them rotten."

Luc and I were reminiscing about the old days when I looked up to find Peter frowning at us from across the room. Well, let him be jealous of this charming foreigner. We could kiss and make up when we got home tonight.

Garrett wandered over and put his arm around me. "Nice party," I told him.

"It was all Thalia's doing," he said, beaming. "Sorry to hear you've been under the weather." I was about to protest when I caught Thalia's warning look.

"Darling," prompted Thalia, "why don't you say a few words to your guests." Garrett needed no encouragement. After getting everyone's attention, he thanked the crowd for celebrating with him. "And now let's raise a glass to our beautiful hostess who organized all this single-handedly." There was much clapping and cheering as Garrett embraced Thalia and gave her a long kiss on the lips. I looked over at Etienne. He had an amused smile on his face.

A few minutes later, Thalia made her way into the kitchen and I followed. "Did you tell Garrett I was sick?" I asked accusingly.

"Yes, he wanted to know why I was off to France again. I said you had bronchitis."

"You could have warned me that I was supposed to be recovering. I wouldn't have worn blush," I said facetiously.

Thalia gave me a quick hug. "Don't you love him?"

It took me a second to realize the topic had switched to Etienne. "He seems very nice. And he's clearly crazy about you."

"I know." Thalia gave a giddy laugh.

"You didn't tell me Luc was going to be here," I said.

"It was a surprise. He wanted to get together in Paris, but I didn't have time."

I bet, I said to myself.

"So he decided to pay me a surprise visit. He arranged it all with Garrett." We rejoined the gathering in the living room, and Thalia floated away to mingle. Pastries were passed around. I was on my second petit four when I felt a hand on my shoulder. It was Luc. "Come outside. It's a full moon."

We stepped through the French doors and strolled out into the moonlit garden, making our way to a bench under a broad magnolia. "Tell me about that magnificent mountain," he said, gesturing toward the double peaks that rose behind us.

"Mount Tamalpais," I said. "The Sleeping Lady. That's what some people say the Native Americans called it. It does look like a reclining woman, doesn't it?"

"Hmm. Not really."

I laughed. "You have to see it from the right perspective. If you look at it from the south in Mill Valley, it's much more apparent. Maybe I can take you on a walk there. It's really spectacular. To be just a few miles from San Francisco and have a place that's left undeveloped like that—it's . . . it's a gift. I've hiked it in the moonlight—with the dog, of course. It's unbelievably gorgeous."

"I'd like that." He smiled. "So how is it working with my sister? Is she as bossy as ever?"

"No, no, it's a good match. She handles the finances, and I'm more the, um, arty one. It works well. So tell me more about your farm," I prompted.

"It's really nothing. Just two hectares—about five acres. Thalia tells me you're quite a gardener yourself."

"Oh, I don't know about that." We spent the next half hour talking about soil amendments, gophers, and the smell of wet earth after a spring rain.

"There you are," said Peter, appearing at the back door. I made the introductions, and the three of us chatted for a bit. Then, stifling a yawn, Peter said, "Sorry to spoil the fun, but I've been up since six. I need to get to bed. We should get going."

"All right. Au revoir," I said to Luc, reiterating my offer to take him on a hike.

As Peter and I were getting our coats, I saw Marcel coming down the stairs from the second floor. "Exploring the house?" I asked.

"I was looking for the loo." He gave me a curt nod and walked back into the crowd.

Sunlight streamed through the filmy curtains as I lay submerged in a mildly erotic dream: I was at a Parisian sidewalk café with Peter. Jasper was there, too, but he was smaller and looked like a potbellied pig. Peter was stroking my bare breasts as I sipped a cappuccino. Befitting the topsy-turvy logic of dreams, none of the other patrons noticed anything amiss as they munched their croissants. I was jolted awake by the reality of Jasper bounding off the bed with a sharp cry of delight. I opened my eyes just in time to see the back end of him disappearing down the stairs.

"Peter?" I called. "Peter?"

"I'm going for a run," he shouted from downstairs. "I'm taking the dog with me."

The clock said eight thirty. I turned over contentedly, burrowing deeper under the covers. This meant I could skip Jasper's customary weekend hike. It was rare that Peter took the dog out. Maybe he was feeling magnanimous thanks to the superb sex we'd had last night following the party. I hoped for a repeat performance when he returned from his run.

I slipped back into a deep sleep, not waking until the phone rang. It was Thalia. "Rae, can you meet me at the farmers market in half an hour?"

Peter still wasn't back. "Um. OK. Sure." So much for my lascivious plans. We arranged to meet at the market's south entrance. I took a five-minute shower, threw on some jeans and a sweater, and left.

I was sampling cherry tomatoes when Thalia showed up. "Here," I said, handing her a stalk of brussels sprouts. "I bought you a present. Since you insist on smoking, you should at least eat more cruciferous—"

"I can't take those home," Thalia interrupted. "I don't want Garrett to know I was here. He thinks I'm at the shop. He'll suspect something."

"Honey, you've been screwing Etienne for a year and a half, and Garrett has been oblivious. Do you really think he's going to open the vegetable bin and figure the whole thing out?"

"Oh, fine," said Thalia sharply, snatching the stalk. With her other hand, she took hold of my elbow and purposefully steered me out of the stream of shoppers. "He left another anonymous note."

"What!"

"Yes, it was on the windshield of my car this morning." Thalia fished around in her Bottega Veneta shoulder bag. "Here."

I looked at the words printed in a shaky hand on plain white paper. *I want $20,000 in cash. Monday evening. 6:30. Enter Golden Gate Park at the corner of 6th Avenue and Fulton Street and take the path to the left. Put the money under the first bench. Leave the park and walk across Fulton Street to the bus stop. Get on the next bus. I will be watching.*

"That's tomorrow," I said. "This . . . this must be a joke. Things like this don't really happen."

"Apparently they do," Thalia said dryly.

"Was your car in the garage last night?" I asked.

"Yes, but the garage doors were wide open. Marcel could have done it when he left the party. That toad. Now that he's been to my house and seen that I have money, he's making his move."

"You have to go to the police."

"Oh, no," Thalia said firmly. "I know how to handle this. I'm going to leave a little package under the bench with a note of my own telling him to go to hell." She stamped out her cigarette.

"How can you be so sure it's Marcel? It could be Etienne's wife, couldn't it? I mean, she can't be too happy about you carrying on with her husband."

"She wouldn't be asking me for money. She's loaded."

"Well, what about their son? He's a big fan of Hollywood movies. And you have to admit this is pretty melodramatic."

"Don't be ridiculous. Julien is a darling young man. We get along very well. It's clearly Marcel, and I'm going to put a stop to it. He's a sniveling little coward. As soon as he gets my note about refusing to cooperate, he'll back off."

"Thalia, this is crazy. Why don't you call the police? Or just tell Garrett. He'll—"

"No!" she snapped. "Let me handle this."

"OK, then at least take your brother with you."

"Leave Luc out of this. I'd rather not involve him. He and I had an argument this morning."

"About what?"

"Oh, it's nothing," Thalia said, looking peevish. "He wants me to agree to sell a piece of property we own together. But it would be foolish to sell. It will only go up in value if we hold on to it. He knows I'm right, but he's too stubborn to admit it."

Runs in the family, I thought.

"Look," she said, "if you're so worried, you should come with me tomorrow."

"No. No way!" I responded angrily. "It's a stupid, dangerous idea, and I'm not going to be part of it. You're on your own. I'm going home."

CHAPTER 3

A handful of the stores along the ten-block stretch that constituted San Anselmo's downtown were having end-of-summer sales, and the street was bustling with people hunting for bargains and enjoying the splendid weather. The tiny shop was crowded with customers, not just browsing, but buying. I was glad we had Susan in today. "Excuse me, is this Quimper?" a middle-aged woman asked, pointing to a pair of figurines in the glass case.

"They're lovely, aren't they?" I said. I took the brightly painted man and woman from the case and turned them over. "They're from the 1940s. Of course, Quimper pottery is still being made today in Brittany, but I just love these vintage pieces."

The woman handled the colorful figures carefully, turning them over, then setting them on the counter side by side. I allowed her to take her time while I turned to help another customer. When I turned my attention back to the woman, she had her credit card in hand. "I'll take them," she said enthusiastically. "You ladies always have the most beautiful items. And it smells so good in here." By the time she walked out the door, she had bought not just the figurines but also two fig-scented French candles at forty-eight dollars a pop.

When I slipped into the back room for more tissue paper, Thalia followed me. "I went to look at the spot last night," she said with the air of one revealing a secret.

"What spot?"

"The bench where I'm supposed to leave the money tonight. I was in the city to meet Garrett for dinner, so I drove through the park and took a look."

"And?" I didn't see the point for this reconnaissance ahead of time. How hard was it to find a bench in the park when the blackmailer had given such explicit instructions?

"Here's what I think," Thalia said. "You should go with me tonight. When I get on the bus and leave, you stay and watch Marcel pick up the package."

"Absolutely not," I said, struggling to pull down a large roll of tissue from the top shelf.

"I was going to do it myself," Thalia went on, ignoring my refusal. "But unfortunately, Marcel is not as stupid as I thought. He chose a pretty good spot for the drop-off. The bench is on a bit of a rise. If he hides in the bushes near there, he'll have a clear view of the bus stop across the road. He'll be able to tell if I don't get on the bus."

"Do you mean you were considering not getting on the bus? You were going to go back and confront him?"

"Of course," Thalia said with a laugh. "Now listen. The bus stop is right in front of a bar. It's called Scotty's . . . no, Smitty's. You'll wait in there. I'll drop off the bag, cross the street, and wait for the bus. As soon as the bus pulls away—with me on it— you dash into the park and catch him red-handed."

"You're delusional."

"Rae, it's so simple."

"I suppose you want me to wear a fake mustache?"

Thalia gave an exasperated sigh. "I just want you to get a good look at him. You don't need to say a word to him. I'll confront him later. You could even snap a picture of him—"

I cut her off. "No. And besides, what makes you so sure he's going to pick up the money right then? What if he doesn't come for it for another two hours?"

"No, he can't do that. He needs to be certain I'm on the bus. If he delays, he risks having me come back to watch for him. Besides," she added, "he wouldn't leave a bag of money just sitting out in public."

"Forget it," I said. "Peter would kill me. Although . . . " I wavered, remembering that Peter would be attending some sort of architectural awards dinner in San Francisco. He wouldn't have to know if I accompanied Thalia to the park.

As I debated, Susan poked her head in and said, "I hate to interrupt, but it's pretty busy out here."

"Sorry!" I said. "Be right there." By the time Thalia brought it up again, I had made up my mind. No way was I skulking around after a blackmailer in Golden Gate Park. I tried one more time to talk her out of going, but she wouldn't budge.

Later that evening, as I stirred the simmering carrot soup, I brooded about Thalia's plan. Perhaps her idea wasn't so bad, I reassured myself. If Marcel was the sort of person inclined to hide behind an anonymous note, maybe a direct confrontation was the best response. I tasted the soup, frowned, and snipped a few more fresh thyme leaves into the pot. The doorbell rang.

Once I had decided to skip the park rendezvous, I'd invited Sonia for dinner. That way I couldn't let Thalia harangue me into changing my mind. "It smells fabulous," Sonia gushed, handing me a bottle of wine. Her coat was damp. "Sorry I'm late. My photo shoot ran long. Plus, it's raining in the city and traffic was a nightmare," she said. The sky was darkening as storm clouds gathered, and I suspected we might get some rain here too. I gave Sonia the job of opening the wine and left the room to hang up her damp coat.

When I came back to the dining room, she said, "You got a call on your cell." I rooted through my purse and dug the phone out. A missed call from Thalia. No message, of course. I called back, got her voice mail, and promptly hung up. I was too annoyed to leave a message. Even though I'd stuck to my guns and refused to go with her, she was managing to ruin my evening.

Sonia and I were laughing about her latest online dating fiasco when my cell phone rang again. "Oh good, you answered," said Thalia cheerfully. "I just wanted to let you know that I'm here. I parked my car a few blocks down from Smitty's at the next bus stop so I can retrieve it. I'm walking into the park now to leave the package."

"Fine. Call me when you're done." I really didn't want a blow-by-blow account. I hung up and turned my attention back to Sonia, who was ladling out the soup. As we started to eat, a gust of wind whipped up the sheer curtains. I got up and closed the dining room window, then pulled the velvet drapes closed over the sheers. The trees outside were bending in the stiff breeze, but the fire blazing in the fireplace kept the house cozy. Yes, it definitely felt like rain.

I was in the kitchen carving the chicken when my cell phone rang yet again. I hurried back to the dining room, glancing at my watch: 6:50. With any luck, Thalia would have left the package and gotten the hell out of there.

"I'm in Smitty's," Thalia said, sounding excited.

"What's going on? Did you leave the package?" I rolled my eyes at Sonia as I spoke.

"Yep, it's there."

"Did you already get on the bus?"

"I told you, I'm in Smitty's."

"I don't understand."

"I've been waiting for the damn bus for twenty minutes, and now of course two showed up at once," Thalia said. "There's a swarm of people out there, and one bus is double-parked next to the other. Plus it's raining, and traffic is a mess. So I decided to take my chances and slip into Smitty's. There's no way anyone across the street in the park could see me." She sounded pleased at her own cleverness. "When the buses pull away and I'm not there, he'll think the coast is clear and go for the money."

"Thalia, don't you dare go back into that park!"

"Relax. I'll call you the instant I'm . . ." Her voice trailed off. "That son of a bitch," she said softly, almost to herself.

"Thalia? Are you still there?"

There was silence at the other end.

"What is it? Did you see him? Did you see Marcel?" Still no response. "Thalia, what the hell is going on?"

"It's nothing," Thalia said.

"Tell me!" I insisted. "Who's there?"

"It's not Marcel. I swear to you, it has nothing at all to do with this. I'll tell you later."

"Thalia—" I began, but she cut me off.

"The buses just pulled out," she said hurriedly. "I have to go." She hung up. I wanted to choke her. I filled my wine glass to the brim.

"Everything OK?" Sonia asked. She had finished the carving

and was setting the platter of chicken on the table, along with the salad.

"Yes, it's just Thalia being a pain in the ass." I raised my glass. "Cheers." As we ate, I was tempted to spill the whole story, but Thalia had made me promise not to mention the blackmail notes. I had told Peter, but it went without saying that spouses told each other everything. That didn't count.

Just before eight, Sonia said, "Sorry to eat and run, but I have to get up at five thirty for a job in Half Moon Bay."

"No dessert? I baked a pie with my neighbor's peaches."

"Cut me a piece to go. I'll eat it tomorrow."

By the time we'd cleared the table and packed up the pie, it was pouring out. "Be careful driving up the hill," I said as we hugged goodbye at the door. I was glad to see Sonia appeared completely sober. Unlike me.

I loaded the dishwasher, wondering how Peter's speech was going. He had practiced it in front of me, and I thought it was quite entertaining. Peter loved being in front of a crowd, so I wasn't worried. As I put away the leftover pie, my eyes landed on a favorite photo, held with a magnet on the door of the fridge. It was a shot I'd taken six years ago. Thalia, Peter, and Garrett gazed at me, windswept and smiling, a cloudless blue sky stretching behind them. Thalia's hand was on the tiller of the sailboat. Peter stood between her and Garrett, one arm around each of them.

I remembered how cold it had been in Sausalito that morning, how Thalia, an accomplished sailor, had given Peter impromptu lessons and had grudgingly admired his quick progress. How Jasper had barked at the seagulls. How the fog had lifted at noon, and the day turned glorious. How we drank too much beer and laughed uproariously. Later, after dinner and more beer, after

Thalia and Garrett had left, Peter kissed me in the parking lot and said, "I think it's time for you to move in."

Now, as I studied Thalia's smiling face, I wondered what made a person stop being in love. I suspected it was a series of small disappointments that accumulated like drops in a jar, until the jar overflowed. Even a big jar had its limits.

Why hadn't Thalia called me back yet? How difficult was it to pick up the phone? I took the pie back out of the fridge and cut myself a hefty slice before dialing her number. After four rings, I got her voice mail. "Thalia, call me the minute you get this," I said. Now my annoyance was morphing into worry as I finished my slice of pie. I was scrubbing the roasting pan when the phone in the kitchen rang. It was Peter. "Hi, honey," he said. "I'm just calling to let you know—"

"When will you be home?" I interrupted.

"Are you OK?" he asked, picking up on the concern in my voice.

"Yes, I'm fine. But I'm worried about Thalia. I think some-thing's happened to her." The words tumbled out. "She was supposed to call me and she never did. She was meeting Marcel at six thirty, and it's already after eight. Do you think I should call the police?"

"The police?" Peter said incredulously. "Of course not. You know how Thalia is. She probably got busy with something else. Maybe she's with her French boyfriend. Look, I have to go back inside. What I wanted to tell you was that my speech was a hit. Thanks for asking," he said dryly.

I felt a pang of guilt. "Oh, Peter, I'm sorry. I want to hear all about it when you get home." We talked for a few more minutes, then I heard my cell phone ringing back in the dining room. I gave Peter a kiss through the phone and hung up. I was too late to get the call, but relief flooded through me as I saw on the display that it was Thalia. Finally. Once again, no voice mail. But at least she'd called.

I immediately called back and left a message insisting that she phone me when she got home, no matter how late. "I don't care if you wake me," I said. "I want to know what happened." Peter was right, I told myself. She was probably with Etienne. After all, he was leaving in just a few days. He and his entourage were staying at a small hotel in San Francisco's Presidio Heights district, just a short drive from the Golden Gate Bridge. Thalia had booked it for them because, she claimed, they'd enjoy being in a charming neighborhood, away from the bustle of downtown. It was more like Paris, she'd said. Renata could stroll to the shops and cafés. "Well, aren't you the accommodating little tour guide," I had commented, suspecting that Thalia had chosen the hotel for her own convenience rather than Renata's.

Yes, I thought, letting out a sigh of annoyance. Thalia must be with Etienne, probably laughing over cocktails at this very moment. I downed the last of the wine in my glass and finished cleaning up.

When Peter finally got home at about eleven, I hugged him with enthusiasm, not caring that he was soggy. "The drive home took forever. It's absolutely pouring," he said, "and I forgot my raincoat at the dinner. I'll have to get it tomorrow."

I released my grip. "So the speech was good?"

"Superb. They laughed in all the right places. I'm dying for a drink."

"I'll get you a glass of wine."

"I'll have you know I got a standing ovation," he said. "I think that calls for a gin and tonic at the very least."

I smiled. "I'll fix it for you."

"Thanks, love. I'm going to run upstairs and take a shower."

I was feeling relaxed now, what with the three glasses of wine and Peter being home. I was still mildly annoyed at Thalia, but that didn't seem so important right now. I stirred Peter's drink and squeezed a slice of lime into the glass. When he came downstairs in his bathrobe, I wondered whether he had underwear on beneath it. As I handed him the gin and tonic, I slipped my other hand inside the robe to find out.

CHAPTER 4

At 2:45 a.m., I woke from a fitful sleep and reached for my phone. Still no message from Thalia. Going back to sleep was out of the question. Peter was softly snoring as I went downstairs to make a cup of tea. Pacing around the kitchen while waiting for the water to boil, I decided it was time to call the police.

Despite my insistence on the phone that something was terribly wrong, the dispatcher sounded unalarmed. She politely took down all the information and promised that patrol cars would keep an eye out for anything unusual in that area of the park. "If your friend doesn't turn up by tomorrow evening, come in and we'll file a missing person's report," the woman told me.

"Thank you," I said as I hung up, although what I wanted to do was scream at this unhelpful woman. Tomorrow evening? Was I supposed to do nothing until then? I paced some more until finally, leaving my tea untouched, I slipped a coat over my pj's, whistled for the dog, and headed to the car. The rain had stopped, leaving behind a fresh scent and sparklingly clear skies. Jasper jumped into the back seat and off we went.

First I drove to Ross and cruised by Thalia's house, hoping to spot her vintage Mercedes. The driveway was empty and the garage doors were closed, so I couldn't tell if her car was in there. All the lights in the house were off.

Now wide-awake and on a mission, I decided to drive into the city. If the police refused to search the area, I'd do it. With a deserted freeway—and my disregard for the posted speed limit— it took only twenty-five minutes to get to Golden Gate Park.

As I hurried along the fog-shrouded path, pulling my thin raincoat tighter to ward off the chill, it occurred to me that traipsing through the deserted park at four in the morning probably wasn't the smartest idea. Not only was it freezing—ah, summer in San Francisco—but the eerie silence was making me jittery. Concern about Thalia already had my stomach in a knot—and guilt, of course. A big helping of guilt. I never should have let her go alone to meet a blackmailer.

A sudden rustling in the bushes startled me. I spun around, casting the wan beam of my flashlight into the shrubbery. Just a raccoon, scurrying away. Jasper hadn't even noticed. He was so delighted at this middle-of-the-night foray that he was trotting along the path, towing me at the other end of his leash.

As the path curved, the bench came into view, illuminated by the hazy glow of a streetlamp. This was where Thalia had been instructed to leave the money. Now, as I reached the bench, I steeled myself for some sign of mayhem. I slowly panned the beam of my flashlight over the area. Nothing. Just a worn bench with peeling green paint. No sign of the package that Thalia had left. No pool of blood. I was flooded with relief that was replaced instantly by weariness. It had been a very long day. I lowered myself onto the bench with a sigh. Thalia was probably at home, fast asleep in her five-hundred-dollar Italian sheets.

All I wanted to do now was crawl into my own bed—preferably without waking my husband. My nocturnal outing seemed ridiculous now, and I certainly didn't want to explain to Peter where I'd been.

I stood up to leave, which the dog took as a cue for more exploring. He lunged into the bushes behind the bench, jerking the leash from my grasp. "Jasper! Bad boy!" I feared he was pursuing a raccoon—or worse, a skunk. Driving home with a dog who stank to high heaven was not how I wanted to end this miserable night. I clomped after him angrily, following him into a clearing behind the shrubbery. "Bad dog!" I scolded again. Jasper was standing stock still, ears flattened, emitting a low growl. I quickly stooped to grab the leash. That's when I saw the body.

It was a scene I knew would be burned into my brain for the rest of my life. Thalia, impeccably dressed, sprawled facedown in the dirt. The remains of an erstwhile homeless encampment littered the spacious clearing—ratty sleeping bags, food wrappers, beer bottles, and cigarette butts—including two Gauloises with Thalia's pearly-pink lipstick staining them. A smashed cell phone lay next to her body, along with her ring of keys. I stood rooted to the spot, trying to make sense of what I was seeing.

I knelt down and shook Thalia by the shoulder, hoping to somehow rouse her. It was only when I rolled the body over that I saw the blood soaking the front of her white raincoat and puddling on the ground. I felt for a pulse but found none. Thalia's skin was cold, so cold. And she had a very odd expression on her mud-streaked face. I remember screaming then, but I'm not sure for how long. Finally, I found the presence of mind to call 911.

Sirens blared as police cars and an ambulance arrived in quick succession. I couldn't help thinking that Thalia would hate to be seen like this, dirty and disheveled. She should be lying on a bed of rose petals, not sprawled in this sordid atmosphere of mud and trash. I had an irrational urge to wipe her face clean, but I didn't. Death was never pretty, but at least it could have some dignity. Thalia's carelessly abandoned body had none.

I was led away from the scene, as police began roping off the area. A woman emerged from a car with photographic equipment, while several others donned white jumpsuits and gloves. They headed toward the roped-off area. A young uniformed officer questioned me for what seemed like an hour, skeptical of my sudden desire to drive to San Francisco in the middle of the night. And being covered in Thalia's blood didn't help. Finally a detective came and spoke with me. After a test of my hands showed that I hadn't fired a gun anytime recently, they finally let me go with the usual caution to stay in town.

I barely remember the ride home, other than the dog sitting beside me in the front seat, happily slurping my face as tears ran down my cheeks.

CHAPTER 5

I lay on the couch, feeling numb. I had no tears left. Just anger—and guilt so strong my chest felt like it would explode. How could I have let Thalia go off alone? Peter sat down and put his arm around me. "Why don't you try going to bed? You've been up all night. I'll wake you when the detectives get here."

"No, I'm OK," I answered unconvincingly.

He stroked my hair. "You should have called me last night. I can't believe you drove yourself home after what happened." That was the third or fourth time he'd said that since I'd walked in the door and awakened him to share the news. But I hadn't wanted to call anyone, not even Peter. By the time the police had finished grilling me, all I wanted to do was get in my car and go home.

The phone rang. It was Luc, sounding distraught. "I'm so sorry you had to be the one to find her," he said. He dismissed my regrets at letting Thalia go to the park alone. "Why wouldn't she go alone?" he asked. "She was probably on her way to meet Etienne."

"So you know about their relationship?" I was surprised. "Thalia told you?"

He hesitated. "No. I just kind of figured it out. It was rather obvious after seeing them together at the party. And Thalia spent a long time getting ready to go out last night, so I just assumed . . . I didn't mention the affair to the police, since that has nothing to do with her getting mugged by some stranger."

"It was *not* a mugging," I said forcefully. I told Luc about the blackmail notes, Thalia's suspicions of Marcel, and her reason for going to the park. He was disbelieving at first but came around when I told him I'd actually seen the notes. He urged me to tell the police, which I certainly planned to do.

Jasper gave a sharp bark as the doorbell rang, and I ended the call with Luc. Peter answered the door, then came into the living room accompanied by two men, one tall and blond with broad shoulders, probably in his midthirties. The second man, who was more portly and looked to be in his midfifties, introduced himself in a gentle voice. "Mrs. Sullivan, I'm Detective Hernandez, and this is my partner, Detective Warren. We're with the San Francisco Police Department." I nodded. "I know you discovered the body last night. We need to ask you a few questions."

"Of course." As Peter and I sat down on the couch, I motioned for them to sit in the two chairs that faced us. Detective Warren took out a notebook and a pen.

"Thalia Holcombe was your business partner?" Detective Hernandez began.

"Yes. And my friend."

"I'm very sorry for your loss." I wondered how often he had to say that to the bereaved. He managed to sound sincere. Maybe he really was sorry, I thought, sorrier than the rest of us, seeing so much death on a daily basis. With a job like that, maybe he was the saddest person in the world.

As he pulled his chair closer to me, I saw cufflinks peeking out from the sleeves of his raincoat. I liked that. I liked that he brought a sense of dignity to his work, this horrible work of dealing with violent death. He was mostly bald, but the hair that remained was jet black and plastered to his head. He had dark, bushy eyebrows and a hint of a five-o'clock shadow on his olive skin, even though it was still morning. He smelled of Old Spice.

"When did you last see Mrs. Holcombe?"

"Yesterday. At the shop we own." Funny how that seemed like weeks ago now. The younger detective wrote in his notebook as Hernandez asked more questions.

"Do you know why Mrs. Holcombe was in San Francisco Monday evening?"

"Yes." Why must they call her Mrs. Holcombe? I wondered. Surely they could call her Thalia. Or would that be too personal?

Hernandez politely repeated his question. "Mrs. Sullivan, we're wondering why Mrs. Holcombe was in Golden Gate Park."

"She went to meet someone who was blackmailing her." The detectives exchanged surprised glances at this bit of information.

Peter quickly said, "Rae, you don't know that."

Hernandez held up a hand. "OK, let's start at the beginning. What makes you think your friend was being blackmailed?"

"She got a note. In France. An anonymous note from Marcel Benoit." Warren interrupted and had me spell Marcel's last name. I continued, "Thalia caught him looking through private papers, and he threatened her."

Hernandez stopped me. "Was the note anonymous, or was it from Mr. Benoit?"

"Both. I mean . . . it wasn't signed. But Thalia showed it to me, and she said it was from Marcel." This was frustrating. "He lives in France. But he's here in the Bay Area." I went on to recount Thalia's suspicions of Marcel. "He's staying at a hotel in the city. You need to go talk to him before he leaves town."

"Let's go back to the note," Hernandez said. "Do you remember what it said?"

"Of course! It said, 'I know about your affair.'"

The detectives looked at each other again. "And did Mrs. Holcombe in fact have a lover?" Hernandez asked.

I hesitated, then nodded. I didn't want them to think of Thalia like that, like someone who had no scruples, someone who got what she deserved.

"What's this person's name?"

"Etienne Duchamp." Before Warren could ask, I spelled it for him. "He's Marcel's boss."

"OK, so Mrs. Holcombe was involved in a relationship with Mr. Duchamp," Hernandez continued. "To your knowledge was her husband aware of this?"

"Oh, no," I said emphatically.

"And the note demanded money?"

"Not that one. But the second note did."

Hernandez took a deep breath. "The second one?"

"Yes, she got it on Sunday." I explained that she'd found it on her car the morning after the party. "This time he asked for money to keep the affair secret." I looked up at Hernandez with impatience. "Don't you see, it had to be one of the people who were here from France."

"And this demand for money was the reason Mrs. Holcombe was in Golden Gate Park?" Hernandez asked.

"Yes, that's what I'm telling you," I said, growing more frustrated. "The note told her where to leave the money. Twenty thousand. But she wouldn't do it. She said she was going to tell him to leave her alone. I begged her not to go. Or at least to take her brother with her. She tried to get me to go with her, but I said no."

"Oh my God," Peter burst out.

"I wish I had, Peter," I said in anguish. "Maybe she'd still be alive."

"Or you could *both* be dead!" Peter said.

Hernandez coughed, and Peter and I fell silent, glaring at each other. Hernandez continued. "This relationship with Mr. Duchamp—you say Mr. Holcombe wasn't aware of it?"

"No, I'm pretty sure he wasn't," I answered.

"And yet Mrs. Holcombe was not overly concerned about this note writer telling her husband about the affair?"

"It wasn't that. Of course, she didn't want Garrett to know. But she wasn't prepared to give in to blackmail. Look, if you knew Thalia, you'd understand."

Warren spoke up. "Is Holcombe a jealous type?"

Before I could answer, Peter said, "He was probably too caught up in his own business to notice anything."

Hernandez said politely, "I need to hear from Mrs. Sullivan right now, sir. When we're finished, we'll have a chat with you." Peter nodded.

Warren continued. "Suppose Mrs. Holcombe told her husband the truth. How do you think he'd react?"

"I have no idea."

Warren looked skeptical. "But you've known him for years. You must have some idea. Suppose she told him about the affair and maybe even about her plan to go to the park. That could have given him the idea to follow her—"

I interrupted him. "Wait, you think Garrett killed Thalia? That's ridiculous! He loved her!"

Hernandez attempted to smooth things over. "We don't have any theories yet. We're just beginning our investigation. We're simply trying to get a better understanding of the situation. And the information you've given us is very helpful."

I sank back against the couch cushions and closed my eyes. How could they think it was Garrett when I'd practically solved the case for them? I had nothing more I wanted to say.

"Look, my wife is exhausted," Peter said firmly. "I think that's enough for now." The detectives agreed that I should come to the police station the next day when I was feeling better. Peter poured me a glass of brandy and ushered me upstairs. "Drink this," he ordered. Although it was only eleven in the morning, I was happy to comply.

I opened my eyes and checked the clock: 5:40 p.m. Why was I in bed? Jasper was curled in a ball next to me on top of the comforter. What day was it? Then I remembered, and my throat tightened.

I stumbled into the bathroom. My head felt like it was stuffed with cotton balls, and an acrid film coated my tongue. I brushed my teeth, washed my face, then brushed my teeth again. When I emerged from the bathroom, Peter was setting a tray on my night table. "I heard you walking around," he said. "I made you some tea."

"Thanks." I had no desire for tea but took a few sips anyway. Suddenly, I realized it was Tuesday. "No one opened the shop today! And I had a customer picking up an order—"

"Relax. Sonia went there early this morning and took care of everything. She put up a sign saying you'll be closed for a week."

"What! Sonia wouldn't do that without talking to me first!"

"She talked to *me*. I told her you're still in shock. You're in no condition to go to work."

"Don't baby me, Peter," I snapped. "I have things to do." I stripped off my sweatpants and T-shirt and started getting dressed. "I'm sure Garrett needs me."

Peter reached out and took hold of my wrist. "Garrett's OK. I talked to him this morning. Rae, this isn't the time for you to take care of everyone. You've had a nasty shock. Give yourself time to recover."

I shook his hand off my wrist. "I *am* recovered! I'm sure Garrett would like some help getting ready for the funeral. And I have to talk to Detective Hernandez," I insisted. "He wants me to come in. You heard him. I need to make sure he understands about Marcel."

"Tomorrow. He said to come in tomorrow." He spoke in a gentle voice as if talking to a not-very-intelligent child, which infuriated me.

"OK, fine. I'm going to call Garrett and then I'm going out for a hike. I need to clear my head."

A half hour later, as I was stepping out the front door with the dog, Peter put his hands on my shoulders and spun me around to face him. "You know that I love you, right?" he asked. "I only want what's best for you." I nodded.

I led Jasper down the brick path and through the front gate. We turned right and set out with no destination in mind. All I knew was that I needed to keep moving because that somehow muted the anger and grief. I breathed deeply, inhaling the smell of approaching fall. Already the sycamores were dropping their leaves, which crunched underfoot, releasing their tangy aroma. It was a smell that never failed to transport me to my grandmother's Brooklyn front porch, shaded by a broad, leafy canopy. This memory had always been a source of comfort, but today it brought a lump to my throat.

After about twenty minutes, we came to the outskirts of Deer Park at the northeast foot of Mount Tam. Jasper was tugging excitedly at the leash, his nose twitching. He knew this place, where there were flowing streams, scampering squirrels, and the occasional horse and rider—all deliciously interesting.

We quickly crossed the flat field near the park's entrance, and, after a few minutes, the trail started to rise, passing through low, scrubby brush. I kept up a rapid pace, not slowing even when my calves began to burn. The path zigzagged up the mountain's steep flank, passing under bay and live oak trees, then through sunny grasslands, until it finally leveled out at a junction of several trails. I paused for a minute, wishing I'd brought water, then pressed on. I was determined to reach the intersection of trails known as Five Corners before turning back.

"Come on, Jasper, we're almost there," I said to the dog, who was losing momentum. At last we reached our destination, a spot that felt like the epicenter of the planet. Utter stillness. No roads, no sound of cars, not a structure in sight. The formerly tawny hills were already sporting a downy, green cloak after just one rainfall. I sat down and gazed into the distance. How could one person murder another? I pondered. Clearly Marcel wasn't a psycho who kills for pleasure. What could Thalia have said that had so enraged him? Had she threatened to go to the police? Maybe he was desperate for money, so desperate that he killed Thalia when she refused to pay.

It wounded me to imagine Thalia suffering or, worse, afraid. I'd never known her to fear anything. A fresh flood of tears started flowing. What right did Marcel have to make Thalia afraid? What right did he have to obliterate my pleasure in the smell of sycamore leaves?

I will punish Thalia's killer, I said to myself. I will expose him, and I will punish him. I rose to my feet, wiped my face, and started down the trail.

CHAPTER 6

The morning commute traffic was heavy on Highway 101 going south. Peter had offered to drive, reminding me that if there were two of us we could use the carpool lane, but I wanted time alone to think. I mentally rehearsed my conversation with Detective Hernandez. I realized that I hadn't been completely coherent when he came to the house yesterday. No wonder he hadn't understood about Marcel.

Today I felt a lot more levelheaded. Plus I was dressed like a grown-up: slim gray skirt, crisp white blouse, and a gold bangle bracelet. I'd even dug out a pair of no-nonsense black shoes I rarely wore because they looked like they belonged to a nun. I was determined to be taken seriously. I envisioned Detective Hernandez nodding sagely as I explained about Marcel.

He and Detective Warren needed to let go of this silly notion that Garrett was involved in Thalia's murder. Poor Garrett. Not only was his wife dead, but the police were also grilling him about whether he knew of her affair, which he'd sworn to me he hadn't when I talked to him this morning. Well, at least Peter had gone over to the house to be with him.

How wrong Thalia had been about Peter, I thought with a

touch of self-righteousness. Years ago, she had tried to convince me that he was a bad bet. Now she'll see, I told myself. Not that I believed in an afterlife. At least not exactly. But part of me was convinced that somehow in death all truth was revealed.

Thalia had called Peter a heartbreaker. "My friends say he's slept with every woman on the Berkeley campus—at least all the straight, pretty ones," she had warned me, taking it upon herself to delve into Peter's reputation after I spent a night with him. It was during our senior year in college. I'd flown in from Madison to visit Thalia at Stanford. She had dragged me to a party in Berkeley, which turned out to be hosted by one of Peter's grad school classmates. My first impression was that this brash, handsome man was entirely too full of himself, but his charm won me over, and I agreed to leave the party and have a beer with him. Many drinks later, we ended up back at his place, an apartment in a converted attic near campus.

The sex was incredible. Really incredible. The next morning, we exchanged phone numbers, and he promised to call me in Madison. He never did. For months, I fought the impulse to call him. He has my number, I told myself. He could call if he wanted to.

After that, all the other men I met seemed lackluster, destined to be no more than friends. "Why don't you at least sleep with one or two of these guys you go out with?" Thalia had urged over the phone, managing my social calendar from afar. "You can't put your life on hold for that arrogant jerk."

"No . . . that doesn't seem fair to them when I know there's no future in it."

"Not fair?" Thalia said. "What planet are you on? Sex with no commitment is every guy's dream."

Thalia, meanwhile, was serial dating. As soon as a guy became loopy over her, she grew bored. "There's no challenge," she complained. "They fall in love with me too easily."

"Boo-hoo," I said. "Frankly, Thalia, I don't know how you do it. Don't you feel even a little bit attached after you sleep with someone?"

"It's like eating," Thalia said nonchalantly. "I like variety. Some men are grilled cheese. Some are chateaubriand. But even with chateaubriand, you don't want it every night."

Why not? I wondered.

Eight years later, after I had moved to San Francisco, I was thumbing through a local magazine, and there was a photo of Peter, looking thinner, his face more chiseled with fine lines around the drop-dead blue eyes. The article was a profile of him and his restoration work that was the talk of the Bay Area.

I looked him up, then nervously dialed his number, rehearsing the message I'd leave. He answered. "Hi. It's Rae Crespi. I met you——"

"Rae with the architect father. And the great ass."

"Excuse me?"

"I remember you. I think about you a lot."

This was certainly moving along faster than I'd expected.

"So I'm guessing you saw the article about me?" he prompted.

"Yes. Very flattering."

"Don't believe everything you read."

I laughed.

"I lost your number, you know," he said smoothly. "I kept hoping you'd call me."

I wasn't sure I believed him, although I very much wanted to. We arranged to meet for lunch at a café on Chestnut Street in the Marina. I arrived late, not wanting to appear too eager. He was sitting at an outdoor table.

"Rae!" He got up as I approached and hugged me. Damn. He was even better looking than I remembered. My resolve to play it cool was quickly evaporating.

We lingered over lunch, catching up on the past few years. I accepted his offer to see his house, which had been featured in the article along with various other projects he'd designed. Zipping over the Golden Gate Bridge in his Porsche with the top down and the sun shining, I felt as besotted as I did eight years earlier. The tour of his house took a detour into the bedroom, where he pulled me toward him and started kissing me. "I was a fool not to call you," he murmured.

After that day, we began spending most of our free time together. When we decided to get married seven months later, most of my friends whooped with excitement. Thalia, though, had her reservations. "You hardly know this guy," she said.

"I know he makes me feel beautiful. He's crazy about me. He's smart as anything and talented. And he helps support his mother, who lives in Oregon."

"All good, I admit. But . . ."

"He's chateaubriand," I told her.

Thalia rolled her eyes. "Sweetie, sex—albeit a marvelous activity—isn't everything. You don't think I married Garrett for the sex, do you? No," Thalia said, answering her own question. "I married him because we're compatible. We like the same things. We like going to the theater and the ballet. We like to travel. We're good doubles partners."

"Oh." To me, this sounded more like a best friend than a husband.

Thalia laughed and squeezed my arm. "You marry your handsome chateaubriand and live happily ever after. I'm just being a curmudgeon. If that's what you want, you know I support your decision. Besides, Garrett likes him. They talk about investments.

My reminiscences came to an end as I turned off Kezar Drive onto Waller Street. TV news trucks crowded the police station parking lot. Reporters and cameramen were set up in front of the building. And a podium with a microphone stood at the bottom of the steps. I exited the lot and searched for a spot on the street. By the time I walked back, the press conference was starting. From the back of the crowd, I watched as reporters peppered the man at the podium with questions.

"First of all, I want to reassure the people of the Bay Area that Golden Gate Park is safe," the man was saying. His prematurely silver hair was in stark contrast to his tanned, unlined face. His tie was loosened, and the sleeves of his crisp white shirt were rolled up. "As I'm sure you're aware, the rate of crime in the park is extremely low, especially for such a well-used facility in a large metropolitan area. That being said, we *have* beefed up park patrols in response to this unfortunate incident." He went on to summarize the known facts of the case, which were few. "Now I'll take questions."

The questions, as well as the answers, were mostly predictable. Yes, the police believed it was an isolated incident. Yes, there were signs of robbery. No comment on what was stolen. No signs of sexual assault.

One reporter asked, "Captain Ryken, do you believe that the victim was killed by someone she knew?"

"As I said, it's still too early to determine the motive for the crime," Ryken responded. "We're looking into all possibilities."

Another reporter asked, "You said there were signs of robbery. Isn't that a motive?"

"That's certainly possible," said Ryken. "But we're not ruling anything out yet."

Yet another reporter pressed the captain for answers: "Given that the mayor is friendly with Garrett Holcombe, will you be fast-tracking this investigation?"

Ryken's mouth tightened, but he quickly hid his annoyance and gazed earnestly into the cameras. "Politics plays no role in any of our investigations. We investigate all homicides with equal vigor. Rest assured that we are devoting all the resources at our disposal to identifying and capturing the perpetrator, as we would with any homicide."

I was doubtful that a homeless man who had his throat slit in a fight would receive the same attention as the well-heeled Thalia Holcombe, but really, what else could Ryken say? I was grateful that the case was receiving so much attention—and that nobody was asking about any extramarital affairs. For now, at least, Thalia's private life seemed to still be private.

The questions continued for several more minutes, then Ryken thanked everyone and went back inside. I waited a moment for the throng to dissipate before walking up the steps. I told the uniformed officer at the desk that I was here to speak with Detective Hernandez but was informed that he was out in the field. "Detective Warren is here, though," the officer told me. "I'll call him for you."

Damn. I was hoping to speak to Hernandez, preferably in private. I could tell Warren didn't like me—and it was mutual. The cop on the phone said, "Rae Sullivan is here to see you." I couldn't hear Warren's response, but I saw a slight smirk cross the officer's face before he said to me, "He'll be right out."

A few minutes later, Warren greeted me cordially, led me into a room, and closed the door. Before I was even in the chair, I said, "I really need to tell you about Marcel. He—"

"Yeah, we'll get to that. But I have a few questions for you first." I was annoyed but nodded in agreement. Warren opened a folder on his desk and scanned the first page. "I see that you and Mrs. Holcombe had life insurance policies on each other."

I gave him a blank look. "What? No we didn't."

"Yes, it seems that you did." He pushed the paper across the desk to me. I read through it, puzzled. "I don't know what this is," I said.

"That's your signature, isn't it?" he challenged.

"Yes . . . but I don't remember any life insurance policies."

"And yet your business has been paying the premiums for three years."

I frowned. "I don't know anything about that. Thalia pays all the bills."

"Well, that's not exactly true," Warren said. "I see that the most recent checks were signed by you on July 22."

"That's because Thalia was out of town," I said indignantly. "I'm telling you, I normally don't pay the bills. I did write a check to the insurance company, but I assumed it was for fire and theft. I don't know anything about life insurance. Thalia handled all the finances."

"But this is your signature, isn't it?"

I wanted to slap him. Here I was trying to help and he was treating me like a criminal. I forced myself to hold my temper. "Yes. It appears I did sign that when we set up the business. But there were so many papers to sign, I really have no memory of it. Garrett handled it all for us. You should ask him."

"Oh, we will. We definitely will."

At that moment, Hernandez came in. "Good morning. Sorry I wasn't here when you arrived." He pulled up a chair and smiled at me—not the condescending smile Warren had given me, but a patient, kindly smile. He gave his partner a meaningful look, and the younger detective left the room.

Feeling encouraged, I took a deep breath, then plunged in: the blackmail note, another note, the rendezvous in the park. Hernandez allowed me recount the whole thing without interrupting, as the video camera recorded it all. I ended by emphasizing how fervently I'd tried to talk Thalia out of going. "I knew it was a bad idea! I told her to at least take her brother with her. She should never have gone there alone."

I was hoping Hernandez would say something absolving me of blame, but instead he said, "Tell me a little more about this first note, the one that said, 'I know about your affair.' You say Mrs. Holcombe received it in Paris at her hotel. Do you know the name of the hotel?"

"Hôtel Sainte Bernadette. It's where she always stays."

"And do you know when she received it?"

"A few weeks ago. It was the day before she flew home. Hold on a minute." I checked the calendar on my phone. "Here it is. August 5. I met her the next evening, and she showed me the note."

"So you actually saw it."

"Yes, of course." Why was he being so skeptical? "It was printed on white paper."

"Do you mean printed by hand, or a printout?"

"A printout."

"What else did it say?"

"Something about paying."

"Did it specify an amount?"

"Oh, no. It was vague. It didn't actually ask for money." I could hear how dumb this sounded. He was probably thinking that wasn't blackmail. Peter had pointed out the same thing. "I know it doesn't sound like blackmail," I said lamely.

"No, no, it's not uncommon for demands to start that way," Hernandez said mildly. "The idea is to throw the person off-balance, make them fearful of exposure before demanding money. Now how did Mrs. Holcombe react to the note?"

"Well, she was positive it was from Marcel," I said with certainty. "She said he was trying to intimidate her."

"Intimidate her how?"

I shrugged. "By threatening to expose the affair, I suppose. Does it matter what he meant?" I felt my annoyance rising. "Someone sent her a note in France, and then a few weeks later, when the people from France arrived, she was killed. Can that just be a coincidence?"

Hernandez said nothing.

"And Marcel was up to something at Etienne's company. Thalia told me she had caught him going through Etienne's private files. He was definitely not trustworthy. Julien—Etienne's son—said so too." This was not going as smoothly as I'd expected. "Look, Marcel is planning to leave San Francisco in four days. Isn't there any way you can keep him here while you investigate?"

"I understand your sense of urgency, and I assure you we're taking this very seriously. Now you say the victim received a second note three days ago. Tell me about that."

I described Thalia's discovery the morning after the party and our meeting at the farmers market. "Don't you see," I said, my voice rising, "it makes perfect sense that it was Marcel. After all, he was in both places when she got the notes."

"So were several other people," Hernandez said quietly. He paused to let that sink in before continuing. "Tell me about the second note. Was it on the same paper as the first?"

"It was just plain white paper. I don't know if it was the same paper. But this one was handwritten. It looked fake, like someone right-handed had written with his left hand or something. It asked for money. Twenty thousand dollars. I don't remember the exact wording. But it described where to drop off the money. It was very specific." I told him about the instructions as best as I could recall, including crossing Fulton Street and getting on the bus.

Hernandez asked more questions, clarifying the details of Monday night. They had examined my phone to get the exact timing of the calls—the first one as Thalia approached the park, the second one from Smitty's, the final missed call at 8:22. We went over the sequence of events several times. I wondered whether he was checking to see if my story changed. Finally, he moved on.

"Can you tell me about any jewelry Mrs. Holcombe usually wore?" he asked.

I was surprised by the question but had no trouble answering. "Her wedding ring. Her tennis bracelet. Usually earrings."

"Tell me about the bracelet."

"It was a tennis bracelet. You know, a row of diamonds linked together. It was an anniversary present from her husband."

"Which hand did she usually wear it on?"

"Her right."

"Are you sure?"

"Positive. She's had it for years. She always wore it on the right. She was left-handed."

"Would she have been likely to have worn it on the night of her death?"

I shrugged. "Maybe. I can't say for sure." I tried to remember whether I had noticed it when I found Thalia's body. I had no memory of the bracelet, but the sleeves of her coat would probably have covered it.

"Do you know of any reason someone would want to murder Mrs. Holcombe?" Hernandez asked.

"I keep telling you! She was being blackmailed." Why wasn't he understanding?

"Blackmailers generally prefer to keep their victims alive," he said wryly.

"But what if she knew who it was? And she confronted him? Then he would want to kill her, wouldn't he?"

"That's certainly possible," Hernandez conceded. "And we're looking into all possibilities."

I looked at him earnestly. "Are you really?" It wasn't a challenge. Just a frank question.

"Yes, yes we are."

His quiet confidence reassured me that he would get to the bottom of this eventually. "Thank you," I said, and I rose to leave, but he wasn't finished.

"I need to ask you about the insurance policy you held against Thalia Holcombe," Hernandez said.

"I already told Detective Warren. I didn't know anything about it. Garrett set up all the paperwork for the business. That must have been his idea. I honestly never gave it another thought."

"I see. Were you and your husband having any financial problems?"

"What? No! Definitely not. You can check my finances. Look at anything you like. I have absolutely nothing to hide!" I walked toward the door. "I need to be going now."

Hernandez stood up. "Thank you for coming in," he said as he held the door open. "You've been very helpful. We'll prepare a statement for you to sign, if you'll just have a seat in the hall." He politely cautioned me not to leave the Bay Area in the coming week without notifying him.

While I was waiting to sign my statement, I overheard Warren saying, "Was I right? I told you that one was going to be a pain in the ass."

But Hernandez came to my defense. "Oh, come on. She's a breath of fresh air. It's nice to meet someone who still believes it's easy to tell the good guys from the bad guys."

Not exactly what I was hoping for, but at least he liked me. Still, he hadn't responded the way I'd hoped, showing no inclination to arrest Marcel. So much for wearing my ugliest shoes.

CHAPTER 7

On a whim, I phoned Julien as I left the police station and invited him to lunch. Although we hardly knew each other, I felt a kinship with him, since he was the only other person in this mess who distrusted Marcel. My hope was that he could tell me something that I could bring to the police, something that would make them take notice. Julien accepted my offer with enthusiasm. "I'd love to get out of here. My parents have been fighting all morning," he said. "I can't stand listening to them."

I drove up Stanyan Street, made a left on Fulton, which bordered Golden Gate Park to the north, and then turned right on Arguello, heading toward Washington Street in the tony Presidio Heights neighborhood. The Victorian and Edwardian homes were painted neutral grays and taupes, muted shades of pale blue and dusty green. The only nod to ornamentation was the gilding on the fretwork of some homes. Black iron railings encased neatly clipped boxwood hedges.

I pulled up in front of the Jameson Hotel, a genteel five-story building from the 1920s that occupied the corner of a residential block. It occurred to me that the hotel was only a ten-minute drive to the scene of the murder. Easy for Marcel to get there and back without anyone missing him. I checked my watch and looked expectantly at the lobby. A slim, stylish woman strolled by, walking a slim, stylish dog.

While I waited for Julien, I phoned my mother. She'd called and left a nervous message this morning, worried that I was about to be gunned down, apparently in some vendetta against San Anselmo shopkeepers. I did my best to reassure her that Thalia's murder had nothing to do with me, but she wasn't convinced. "Take some time off and come back home for a little while," she said.

"Ma, I *am* home." I reminded her that I had a husband and a business to attend to.

"Well, maybe I could take some time off from work and come there," she offered.

The idea of my middle-aged mother in her heels and power suits shadowing me made me chuckle. "Please relax. Talk to Daddy. He'll tell you there's nothing to worry about." At that moment, Julien emerged from the hotel, dressed in a lilac polo shirt and skinny jeans. He climbed into the front seat. "Ma, I've got to go. I love you."

I pulled out and headed toward the Mission District. I'd promised Julien the best burrito in the city, and he'd jumped at the offer, as eager to be part of my sleuthing efforts as he was to sample the carne asada from La Cumbre.

"Parents!" I said. "They mean well, but they can be annoying."

"Yeah. My mother is angry because my father made her come on this trip, and now they're stuck in a murder investigation. We all have to go to the police station at two o'clock to make our statements. She said this is the worst vacation she's ever had."

Hmm. Thalia had said it was Renata's idea to tag along and bring Julien. At least that's what Etienne had told her. Now, according to Julien, it had been Etienne's idea. Why? I wondered.

Why would he want his family in tow when he was visiting his mistress?

We parked on Mission Street near Seventeenth, and I put a handful of coins in the meter. As we walked one block north, Julien was fascinated by the colorful shops, with their wares displayed out front. "This doesn't look anything like the rest of San Francisco!" he said. Here the Victorians were painted lively purples, lime greens, and cobalt blues. The streets were crowded with mothers and young children doing their shopping.

We turned right on Valencia Street, which was hipper, more gentrified, with vintage furniture stores and lots of twenty-somethings dressed in black. At La Cumbre, we joined the line and ordered our burritos and watermelon aguas frescas, then sat at a table up front where we could watch the street scene.

They called our number in a few minutes. Julien unwrapped his burrito eagerly and dove in, making noises of pleasure. When he came up for air, he said, "So do you think Marcel killed your friend?"

"What? Why would you say that?"

Julien shrugged. "He's sneaky. And he didn't like Thalia. I heard him call her a *putain*."

"A whore? He said that to her?"

"No, not to her. He said it when she wasn't there. Because she tried to get him fired."

"What do you mean?"

"She told Papa how she caught Marcel looking through his desk. But my father just laughed about it. He said Marcel was probably putting something away. I think Thalia was right, though, because I also caught him when I was working there during the summer." He went on to tell me how he walked into Etienne's office and found Marcel beside an open file drawer, a folder in his hand. "When he saw me, he stuffed some papers back in and shoved the folder back into the drawer. He had a guilty look on his face."

I wondered how much of this was Julien's imagination. After all, Marcel did work there. Why *wouldn't* he be looking at files?

My skepticism must have been obvious, because Julien said, "You don't believe me, do you? But I'm sure he was snooping. I looked in the file later—it was an orange folder, so I could tell which one it was. It was about shipments from Kenya to the company's warehouse in Marseille. I told Papa, but he laughed at me. He said I watch too many movies. So I made him check the folder. He said nothing was missing."

"Maybe you were mistaken."

"No. All the papers in the folder were in date order, except the four sheets at the front." He paused to take another bite. "I think those were the ones Marcel stuffed back in when I came in the room. And they were all about container shipments from Africa. Why would he be looking at those? He works on business in Asia."

"OK, maybe you're right. And you think Thalia knew?" That would explain why he didn't want her hanging around with Etienne. I decided to tell Julien about the notes Thalia had received. His eyes grew wide.

"Blackmail!" he said breathlessly. "Just like in *The Man Who Wasn't There!*" At my puzzled look, he explained, "It's a Coen brothers classic."

"Oh."

"We have to find out where Marcel was on Monday night," he said excitedly. "I saw him get back to the hotel at about seventeen thirty." He quickly translated for me. "Nine thirty. I was down in the lobby and I saw him get out of a taxi. It was after I came back from dinner with Jerome."

"You and Jerome went out? What about your parents?"

"Oh, my father was too tired after he got back from visiting a rug dealer in Sausalito. He said there was a lot of traffic, and he had gotten lost. He just wanted to take a shower and watch TV. So he and my mother ordered room service. And I went out with Jerome.

"Anyway," Julien went on, "when I got back, I was hanging around downstairs, and that's when I saw Marcel get out of a taxi. He was in a big hurry to get back upstairs. Maybe Thalia found out some secret about him, and that's why he killed her."

Looking through papers, disliking Thalia, taking a taxi. Not exactly proof of homicide. I wondered if my account to the police sounded as far-fetched to them as Julien's theory did to me. Evidence was what I needed, not hunches.

We finished our lunch and arrived at the police station with five minutes to spare. "I'm first on the list," Julien said. "They're taking us one at a time—except for me. They said my mother needs to go in with me since I'm less than eighteen years old."

As we said goodbye and he thanked me for lunch, an idea occurred to me: Marcel's hotel room would be empty while he was being questioned. I asked Julien for the room number and decided to go have a look around.

CHAPTER 8

I rode the elevator to the hotel's fourth floor. My plan was to cajole a maid into letting me into Marcel's room, saying I'd forgotten my key. But a linen cart was in the hall in front of Room 406, two doors away from Marcel's room. Had the cleaner already been in there, or was she heading that way? I decided to hope for the best. After about ten minutes, the maid emerged and opened the door of the next room. Good. She was headed in the right direction. I tried to look purposeful as a couple passed me in the hall. I walked briskly past them and turned the corner, waited a minute, then came back and waited some more. After another fifteen minutes, the maid emerged and wheeled her cart toward Marcel's room. She gave a brisk knock, then unlocked the door and went in, leaving the door ajar.

I debated. I could sneak in and try to hide inside until the maid left. But what if there was no place to hide? I decided to be brazen. I sauntered in with a cheery hello.

"Good afternoon, ma'am," the stout woman said. "I'll be about twenty more minutes."

"Oh, that's all right. I need to make a phone call. Just go ahead with whatever you're doing."

If she thought anything was amiss, she didn't show it. She

got her spray bottle and cloths from the cart. In a moment, the odor of bleach wafted from the bathroom. I sat on the bed pulling open the nightstand drawers. Gideon Bible. Notes scrawled on the pad: a few phone numbers in France. An address on Grant Avenue that I copied onto a scrap of paper in my purse. Noticing a jacket over the back of the chair, I rifled through the pockets. Just some loose change.

The maid came out to retrieve some more items off her cart, then disappeared back into the bathroom. I walked over to the closet. There were a few shirts and pairs of slacks hanging there. It took only a moment to feel in all the pockets. Again, nothing significant, just some coins, a book of matches, and a few receipts. I scanned the receipts: two for Yellow Cab, one for coffee and a croissant at Shaky Grounds, one for a map of San Francisco purchased at a nearby bookstore. Shoving the receipts in my pocket, I moved to the dresser and slid open the top drawer quietly. I poked around the socks and underwear, being careful not to disturb anything. Underneath the folded underwear was a sheaf of papers. I leafed through them quickly, then took a picture of each one with my cell phone and placed them back where I'd found them.

I turned my attention to the drawer below. A few neat stacks of folded shirts. I felt underneath them. Nothing. As I was opening the third drawer, my phone rang, causing me to let out a little yelp. I was definitely on edge, even though I figured I probably had at least forty-five minutes before Marcel made it back. The maid poked her head out of the bathroom. "You all right?" she asked.

"Yes, I'm fine. My phone startled me. I didn't know it was turned up so loud."

Satisfied, she returned to her cleaning. It was Sonia on the phone. I told her I couldn't talk and promised to call later. Then I turned down the volume on the ringer and stuck the phone in my pocket. As I was searching the middle dresser drawer, the maid came out of the bathroom. "I'll do the bed now, ma'am."

"Thanks." I went into the bathroom and closed the door. Now what? I examined the pockets of the bathrobe hanging on a hook. Empty. That was it. I didn't want to go back to the dresser drawers with the maid out there. I paced the small bathroom, waiting. Conscious that I'd been in there a while, I flushed the toilet to add a note of realism.

Now the vacuum was running. I turned on the bathtub and started to fill it. I'd pretend to take a bath until the maid left and then have one last look. After a few minutes, I shut the water off and listened. No sounds of vacuuming. I stepped out of the bathroom. The bed was made, everything tidy.

I ran back to the dresser and started rifling through the clothes. More shirts, sweaters—Aha! A manila folder. I was beginning to read through the papers inside when I heard the click of a key card in the lock. Maybe the maid had forgotten to do something. Then I heard voices. That was no maid. Marcel was talking to Jerome. How had they come back so soon? I hurriedly shut the drawer, grabbed my purse, and dashed into the bathroom. I started to close the door behind me but had the presence of mind to realize that would be a giveaway that someone was in there. Sweeping aside the shower curtain, I stepped into the tub and pulled the curtain closed.

Great. I was standing in five inches of lukewarm water with my shoes on. Not daring to risk the noise of letting the water down the drain, I strained to hear what was going on. "OK, *à plus tard*," Marcel said.

The outer door closed, and after a minute the TV switched

on. Oh God, he was settling in. OK, I'd text Julien and tell him to get Marcel the hell out of there so I could make my getaway. I had just started typing when, to my horror, Marcel walked into the bathroom. I held absolutely still behind the shower curtain.

I could hear him peeing. Then the toilet flushed and the sink turned on. As soon as I heard him walk out of the room, I texted Julien: *I'm hiding in Marcel's bathroom. You have to get him out of the room.*

No response. I waited a few minutes, then texted him again. Nothing. Dammit, where was he? All I could do was hope Marcel wouldn't come back into the bathroom or, worse, decide to take a shower. I imagined him pulling open the curtain and both of us screaming. Finally my phone lit up with a text: *I'm on my way back to the hotel with my parents.*

This could take a while. The water around my ankles grew cold. I could hear Marcel opening and closing drawers. Then his phone rang and I heard him talking, although I couldn't make out what he was saying. I wondered if he might be so engrossed in his conversation that I could make a run for it. No, that would be crazy. Finally, after another twenty minutes, there was a knock on the door. I could hear Julien trying to persuade Marcel to go up to the rooftop pool with him. That went on for a few minutes. Then Julien said, "My mother told me not to go into the pool alone. Just come up and sit nearby. You don't have to swim." Marcel apparently agreed because after another minute, the TV was turned off, and I heard them leave. The door closed loudly behind them.

Stiffly, I stepped out of the tub, my shoes sloshing. I swished the bathmat over the puddle on the floor, let the water down the drain, and bolted out of the hotel room. Running for the stairwell, I hoped Marcel wouldn't notice the wet trail on his carpet.

CHAPTER 9

I called Hernandez first thing the next morning. After three rings, his voice mail kicked in. I groaned in frustration. At the beep, I explained that I'd found some important information and urged him to call me back right away.

I did the breakfast dishes and wiped down the kitchen counters. No call yet. Bursting with nervous energy, I emptied the refrigerator, making the just-cleaned countertops sticky. No matter. I could clean them again. I filled the sink with hot water and soap, put on rubber gloves, and began sponging down the inside of the fridge.

Peter came into the kitchen and poured himself a second cup of coffee. "What's all this?" he asked with amusement.

I brushed back the hair from my sweaty forehead and said curtly, "I'm waiting for a phone call."

"From who, Martha Stewart?" I refused to smile, even though I privately admitted his remark was funny. "OK, I won't get in your way," he said. "But you know Fiona is coming tomorrow. She'll happily clean the fridge."

"Fiona does a fine job, but it's not the same as the person who has to live in the house, is it?" I felt rather mature saying this, although it was patently untrue. Fiona, a motherly middle-aged woman who had cleaned Peter's house since before I came on the scene, put my domestic skills to shame. Peter refilled his coffee cup and retreated back upstairs to his office, no doubt wondering at my newfound commitment to domesticity.

The refrigerator was shining, the countertops were cleaned for the second time, and I was considering tackling the stove when Julien called, saving me from further housework.

"Detective Warren showed me his gun," he said excitedly before I had even finished saying hello. I smiled despite myself. How could I fault Julien for enjoying this whole mess? After all, he'd hardly known Thalia. "So how did the interview go?" I asked.

He launched into a detailed account, starting with the detectives' questions about his age and where he lived. Clearly, being interrogated by the police was a high point of his visit to the States. "They asked me about where I was that night, where everyone was—Marcel, Jerome, my parents. I made sure to tell them about Marcel getting out of the taxi.

"My mother kept trying to answer for me, but the police made her be quiet. She wasn't happy about that. Then they asked me about—how do you say—anonymous notes. Whether I knew about any notes that Thalia had received. That's when my mother spilled her water and we had to stop while it got cleaned up. Anyway, I told them I didn't know about any notes. I wasn't sure if I should say you told me. So I said maybe they should ask you, since Thalia would have told you. That's when my mother started questioning me about why I was spending time with you. The police made her be quiet again."

Julien continued with more details: how the detectives asked if he knew about his father and Thalia, when it had started, and so on. "Oh, and they asked about whether I had gone outside during the party at Thalia's house. And about everyone else, too. Not out back but out front."

This was good news. Maybe they were looking into who might have left the note on Thalia's car. "Did you talk any more about Marcel?"

"I told the detectives I didn't trust him, that I saw him spying on my father's business. Then my mother said, 'Don't be ridiculous.' That's when Detective Warren told her she'd have to leave the room if she interrupted again. I could see she was really mad, but she didn't say anything. I told the detectives that Marcel and Thalia hated each other.

"Good!"

"Maybe." He sounded doubtful. "I hung around in the hallway when it was Marcel's turn to be interviewed. When he came back out, they all shook hands and the detectives thanked him for his help. And Marcel was smiling."

"Crap! He's got them completely fooled." I had been hoping they'd lead him out in handcuffs. "Listen, I saw some papers in Marcel's room," I told Julien. "Some I photographed—they were the itinerary for a trip to Hong Kong. There was another stack, though, that I didn't have a chance to read through or take photos of because Marcel came back. I saw something about a Legrande Warehouse in Marseille."

Julien said that was one of the two warehouses in Marseille that Etienne's company used for receiving shipments. He promised to investigate when he got home, and we said goodbye.

I stepped out the door into the garden and began cutting herbs for dinner. The basil was growing like mad. I decided to make pasta with pesto for Garrett. And a salad with the Indigo Rose tomatoes and some fresh mozzarella. The phone rang.

"Hello, Mrs. Sullivan. I understand you have some news for

me," Hernandez said. He listened as I explained my find. Then he asked, "Where exactly did you discover these papers?"

"In Marcel's hotel room."

"When were you in Mr. Benoit's hotel room?"

"Um . . . yesterday. I went to talk to him, but the maid was cleaning his room so I waited inside."

"And you looked through his personal papers?"

I had no choice but to confess. "Yes! Don't you see, he's about to leave the country! I had to do something. Maybe it's not legal for *you* to snoop in his room, but it's not a crime for me to take a look, is it?"

"Actually, it is, but that's not my primary concern. If he's someone you suspect of being involved in your friend's death, your actions could be very dangerous."

Did this mean he was taking my claims seriously? "Thank you for the warning," I said, "but I just feel like time is running out—and I had to do something."

"I assure you we are investigating every avenue. There's no need for you to put yourself in jeopardy. Do you understand?" he asked with concern.

"Yes."

"Very good." Seemingly satisfied, he listened as I told him whatever I could remember about the papers I'd seen and gave him the address on Grant Avenue.

"You'll investigate that address, won't you?" He didn't answer. I asked again.

"If we think that it has a bearing on the case, yes, certainly." He urged me again to be careful and promised to be in touch if he had any news.

I went back to the garden and started deadheading roses furiously, snapping off spent flowers with my bare hands until a thorn plunged deep into my thumb. "Shit!" I went into the kitchen to rinse off the blood. Peter was making another pot of coffee.

"What happened to you?" he asked.

"Hernandez," I grumbled. "He's not taking anything I say seriously."

"Honey, he seems very capable. Why don't you leave it all to him?"

"Peter, he didn't care about what I . . . what Julien found in Marcel's hotel room." I'd caught myself just in time. I was pretty sure that Peter would not approve of my sneaking into Marcel's room. "There was stuff about Etienne's business. Julien was hesitant to phone Hernandez about what he found, so I did." I noticed that lying was becoming increasingly easy. "But he's not listening!"

Peter sighed, then said, "Look, how about we go away for a few days, since the shop is closed anyway? We'll drive up the coast to that B and B you like."

"Peter, the funeral is in two days!"

"After the funeral, then?" He put his arms around me. "It will do you good to get away."

"OK. Maybe. Let me think about it."

He kissed my forehead and left the kitchen. The last thing I wanted to do was leave town right now, but Peter was being so considerate. I had to stop snapping at him.

I pulled into the familiar circular driveway in Ross. Thalia's convertible sat in the open garage. For a brief instant I felt a pang of anticipation at seeing her. Then I remembered. Thalia was gone. Luc answered the door. "How are you holding up?" he asked.

"Good. Are you OK?"

He nodded. "Garrett's not back yet. Come have some coffee. And that basil smells divine."

I set out ingredients on the kitchen counter: basil, salad greens, and tomatoes, plus pine nuts, a head of garlic, a box of tagliatelle pasta, a hunk of parmesan, two lemons, and a bottle of Montepulciano, my favorite Italian wine. "I didn't bring olive oil," I said. "I'm sure there's plenty here."

He came over to inspect. "Ooh la la. Sweet basil *and* Thai basil."

I smiled. "I couldn't decide which one to use for the pesto, so I brought both."

He put the stems of basil in a glass of cold water to stay fresh, then poured the coffee and set the cups on a tray along with spoons, cream, and sugar. I followed him into the breakfast room off the kitchen. Luc stirred sugar into his black coffee and said, "I'm glad you're here. I'm worried about Garrett."

I nodded in agreement.

"Did he tell you about the gun?" Luc asked.

At my look of surprise, Luc explained that the police had asked if Garrett owned a gun when they came to the house after the murder. "Of course, they must have already known," Luc said, "since it was registered. Anyway, they asked to see it. Garrett went to get the box from his desk drawer—and it was empty."

"Oh no."

"Garrett told them he never locked the door to the study, since there were no kids in the house. They seemed dubious that someone had stolen it."

I wondered if Marcel had pilfered the gun at the party. It

would have been easy for him to disappear for a while and snoop. In fact, I'd seen him coming downstairs from the second floor.

"Yeah, it doesn't look good," Luc continued. "Especially since it was the same sort of gun that my sister was shot with. A 9mm Glock. Although that doesn't mean anything," Luc said, trying to look optimistic. "It's a common sort of gun among you Americans, I'm told."

I bristled. Is that how the rest of the world saw us? As a bunch of gun-toting crazies? This wasn't the Wild West anymore. "Their house was burglarized a few years ago," I said stiffly. "I'm sure that's why Garrett had the gun."

Luc shrugged. "Anyway, the next day was worse. Garrett was called in to the police to explain why he withdrew ten thousand dollars in cash two days before the murder."

"That's a big chunk of money! What did he tell them?"

"Just that it was a personal matter. He refused to say what it was for." Luc shook his head. "He told me it was none of their business. It's almost like he's daring them to arrest him. Seems very foolish to me."

"He's not thinking clearly. I'll talk to him over dinner."

Garrett got home at around four thirty and immediately poured himself a scotch. He looked like he hadn't slept in days. "Thanks so much for coming, Rae. It's been lonely around here without Thalia," he confessed. "Not that Luc hasn't been a tremendous help," he added quickly. "We wrote the obituary for the newspaper together."

Garrett and I spent about a half hour discussing details of the funeral: flowers, catering for a reception back at the house, accommodations for out-of-town guests. I took copious notes as we talked. "OK, I'll make all the arrangements," I told him. "You go relax until dinner's ready."

"Thanks, Rae. I think I'll go lie down. Oh, will Peter be joining us for dinner?"

"No, he's got some work to do." Which was true. But I hadn't exactly invited him.

As Garrett was heading upstairs, he turned and said, "Oh, damn, I still haven't paid the twins who did the valet parking. I got the cash out for them days ago."

"I can do it," I offered. "Where do they live?" This would give me a chance to ask them if they'd happened to see anyone leave a note on Thalia's windshield.

"Are you sure you don't mind? They live just a few blocks away. They've worked for us before when we've had big parties. Nice kids." He pulled out his wallet and started peeling off bills.

I pocketed the cash, scribbled down the address, and promised to stop by their house on my way home. Then I went into the kitchen to start the pesto. Luc had rolled up the sleeves of his blue chambray shirt and was washing dishes. As I chopped garlic, I found myself stealing surreptitious looks at his muscular, tanned forearms working in the suds.

"I'll make the salad," Luc offered. He began rinsing the greens I brought. "Lovely," he said, admiring them. I told myself that the pleasure I felt at this praise was because he was a professional grower admiring my crop. His arms had nothing to do with it.

About forty-five minutes later, we sat down to dinner in the dining room, the three of us clustered at one end of the long table. Luc ate heartily, while Garrett picked at his food despite saying it was delicious. Finally, he brought up the subject I'd been wondering how to broach. "The San Francisco police seem to think I murdered my wife," he said, going to the bar for a refill of his scotch. Luc and I made appropriately scoffing noises and said how ridiculous that notion was.

Garrett sat back down and told me about the missing gun. "I didn't keep the drawer locked—after all, it's not like we had kids in the house. So anyone could have slipped upstairs and gone into my office. There were quite a few people at that party that I'd never met before. Really, it could have been anyone." Like Marcel, I thought, but didn't say so.

"Problem is," Garrett said, beginning to slur his words ever so slightly. "Problem is, my alibi is not solid. Not like Luc here, who was talking to our neighbor at five minutes to eight, so he couldn't have gotten to the city in time to kill Thalia. No, my alibi didn't satisfy the cops."

Luc and I quickly glanced at each other. "What do you mean?" I asked.

"I was at a friend's house from six to nine thirty—except when I went to pick up takeout Chinese food."

"So what?"

"His house is on California Street. And I went to Five Happiness on Clement and Sixth Avenue. I have a receipt," he added petulantly. He swallowed more scotch. "That bastard Warren kept harping on why I chose that restaurant. 'So you just got a sudden urge for kung pao chicken right around the time your wife was being shot,' he said. Smug son of a bitch. I always go to that place. They know me. Warren says it was close enough that I could have driven to the park, shot Thalia, and come back to my friend's house without being gone very long."

Again, Luc and I made appropriate noises of disbelief.

"The autopsy put the time of death between six and ten. But from Thalia's phone calls to you, they were able to narrow it even more." Garrett shook his head sadly. "I understand the good-cop, bad-cop technique. But that doesn't make it any easier to take."

"Garrett, maybe you should tell them what the money was for," I suggested.

A dull red flush spread from his jaw up to his cheeks. "Who told you about that?" he demanded angrily.

"I did," Luc quickly said. "Sorry if it was supposed to be confidential."

"Damn right it was. Rae, forget you ever heard anything about that." He pushed his chair back and stood up, a bit unsteadily. "I'm going upstairs." He stopped in the archway and turned toward us. "Thanks for dinner."

I cleared the table and Luc started on the dishes. "I'm so sorry that Garrett snapped at you," he said. "I didn't realize it was such a sensitive subject. Since he told me about it, it never dawned on me that he'd keep it from you. After all, he barely knows me."

I assured him there was no need to apologize. "But if they think Garrett hired someone to kill Thalia, then what's all that about him going to the park himself to do it?"

Luc shrugged. "Maybe they think he was going to pay someone, then decided to do it himself. Who knows?" When the dishes were all put away, I gathered up my things and Luc walked me to the door. "Let me know if you need any help with funeral arrangements," he said. I promised I would.

CHAPTER 10

I found the twins' low-rise apartment building without too much trouble. Ringing the bell of Unit 3A set off furious barking from within. A pretty forty-something woman answered. "Can I help you?" she asked, peering out from a barely opened door.

I introduced myself and explained that I was there to drop off Garrett's payment to the boys.

"Oh, come in, come in," she said. As soon as the door opened wider, an overweight bulldog waddled out and began growling at me. "Denise! Stop that, Denise!" the woman scolded, to no effect whatsoever. "I'm Margaret," she told me, waving me into the living room. "Have a seat." She gestured toward the couch. I sat down, and Denise stood at my feet, glaring at me balefully.

"I'm so, so sorry about Thalia," Margaret said. "She was such a lovely person. I know her and Garrett from our church. The boys did odd jobs for them sometimes."

"Are the boys at home?"

"No, but they should be back any minute. They're at a friend's house watching the game. Would you like some coffee?"

I said yes, hoping that when she left the room, Denise might follow. Not a chance. The dog immediately jumped up on the couch, continuing to stare at me. A string of drool was form-ing in the corner of her orthodontically challenged mouth. As I shifted my position, the low growling resumed, making the drool quiver.

"Here you are," Margaret said, coming back into the room with two cups of coffee. I reached for my cup, causing Denise to utter a warning bark. Apparently I wasn't allowed any refresh-ment. Margaret sat down in the armchair and smiled at the dog. "She's taken a liking to you. She doesn't usually sit next to strang-ers." Lucky me.

"Such a tragedy about Thalia," Margaret said, shaking her head ruefully. "What a shame that you have to fear for your life if you go into the city at night. It's so dangerous in Golden Gate Park with all those vagabonds lurking about." I nodded, although it seemed to me that confronting a blackmailer was not a good idea regardless of the locale. Meanwhile, Denise contin-ued watching my every move.

"How's poor Garrett holding up?" Margaret asked.

"Oh, as well as you'd expect."

"I'm going to make him a casserole tomorrow. Do you think he'd like that?"

I assured her that he would. Finally, the boys came home and introductions were made. Joshua and James thanked me for bringing the money. "Tell Mr. Holcombe we're sorry about his wife," Joshua said. "Yeah," echoed James. But I could tell the finality of Thalia's death didn't really register with them. Nor should it. They barely knew Thalia.

"Mr. Holcombe told me you boys do a great job for him," I said. "It must have been hard that night, with so many people arriving."

"It wasn't too bad," one of them said. I'd already forgotten which twin was which. "We got to drive some super-cool cars. There was a Jaguar and three BMWs."

"And five Porsches," added his brother.

"Mrs. Holcombe's car is pretty nice too," I said.

"For sure! It's a classic," said twin number one.

"Did you happen to notice anyone hanging around it? I saw that the garage doors were open."

"Oh, Mr. Holcombe left them open for us, so we could sit inside and watch TV while we waited until the guests started leaving." His brother nodded. "We watched an awesome soccer match! Mrs. Holcombe's brother came out to bring us food, and he watched for a while too. He said he didn't want to go back to the party, but he had to."

"Someone left a note for Mrs. Holcombe that night. Whoever it was left it on the windshield of her car. Any idea who that might have been?"

One of the boys shrugged and shook his head. The other said, "No, I didn't see anyone leave a note. But it got really busy at the end. We had a lot of cars to move to let people out."

"Do you remember anyone hanging around, asking you about Mrs. Holcombe's convertible?"

"Yeah, a couple of people. One guy admiring it asked if I knew what year it was. And then there was someone who asked me whose car it was."

"Oh, who was that?"

More shrugging.

"Did he happen to have a French accent?"

The boys both frowned. "I don't think so," one said. "Yeah, I don't really remember," said the other.

"Do you remember what kind of car he came in?"

They both thought for a moment. "I think a Taurus," said

twin two. He turned to his brother. "Or were they the ones in the Hyundai?"

"They? Did he arrive with a group?" I asked.

"Yeah, I think so."

That's all I was able to get. Margaret came back in the room and instructed the boys to take the dog out. I stood up to go, too. As I brushed past Denise, she tried to sink her teeth into my left ankle. Fortunately, I had boots on under my jeans, and I only felt a pinch. None of the family appeared to notice.

CHAPTER 11

Jasper joyously pursued a golden retriever who had a stick in her mouth, the two dogs splashing through the shallow waves and sending up sprays of water with their tails. Sonia and I sat nearby in the sand, letting the tide lap at our toes. I realized I had gone an entire hour and a half without thinking of Thalia—a first in the four days since the murder.

The sun, the breeze, the spicy sent of the nasturtiums trailing down the hillside behind me all enveloped me in a soothing, familiar cocoon.

"How'd you find this spot?" Sonia asked. "I didn't even know it was here."

"Someone at the dog park told me about it. It's nice, isn't it?"

The little beach—which had no name as far as I knew—was at the bottom of a flight of wood stairs. Up above was a quiet street lined with quaint older homes. An idyllic setting, with a view of the water and the Richmond Bridge spanning the bay. The only thing that kept real estate prices in check in this cozy hamlet at the eastern edge of Marin was the fact that its main street dead-ended at the gates of San Quentin prison. The fortress-like building held the largest collection of death-row inmates in the country. On the rare occasions that an execution was scheduled, the streets filled with news cameras and death-penalty protesters engaged in candlelight vigils.

"Do you think the death penalty is a deterrent?" I asked.

"Maybe, if you're planning to kill someone," Sonia mused. "But if you do it in the heat of the moment, no. You're not thinking about the consequences. Of course, murderers who plan it don't expect to be caught. They think they're too clever for that. Otherwise they wouldn't do it. Let's face it. If you believed you could get away with it, don't you have someone you'd like to kill? I know I do."

"I wouldn't mind seeing Marcel suffer a painful death."

Jasper and his pal had demolished the stick by this time, and he was getting bored. He trotted over and graced us with a big shake of sandy wetness. We jumped up laughing. "Let's go this way," I said. At the far end of the beach were more stairs that climbed to a grassy knoll. We stood there awhile, admiring the view all the way from Mount Diablo in the east to Mount Tam, which loomed to the west. We had a bird's-eye view of the San Quentin prison yard, encircled in barbed wire and punctuated with a watchtower and searchlights.

"I think the way to do it is to make it look like an accident," Sonia continued. "Say you want to bump off your nasty, rich husband. You go cross-country skiing out in the backcountry, you get him alone at the edge of a cliff, and wham. Done."

"No wonder you're still single."

"Hey, I'm not advocating it. I'm just saying if it looked like an accident, the police wouldn't ever hunt you down."

"Well, the San Francisco police don't seem to be hunting anyone down," I said ruefully. "Julien told me they were super friendly with Marcel and thanked him for his help! It's hopeless."

"Oh, I don't know. That Hernandez guy seems pretty smart to me."

"You think so?"

"Absolutely. He asked me some shrewd questions."

"Like what?"

"Like about the party at Thalia's. Whether Renata seemed to know what was up."

"And what did you say?"

"That she'd have to know unless she was blind."

"You think he suspects her?" I asked.

"I think he suspects everyone for now. Probably even you."

"Me?" I was offended. "How could he think . . ."

"That's his job. Guilty until proven innocent. Don't worry; he'll sort it all out. I'm telling you, he's shrewd. He even asked me about you and Luc. How long you'd known each other and stuff like that."

"Really?"

"Yes. Speaking of not being blind, I noticed you were doing some heavy-duty flirting at the party."

I blushed at the memory of the fluttery feeling that had lodged in my chest while I was talking to Luc. "Don't be silly. He's an old friend," I said. "I was happy to see him. And I was a little drunk."

"Yeah, there was a lot of that going around. Lover-boy Etienne kept hitting on me."

"What? No! He was in love with Thalia!"

Sonia raised one eyebrow. "I'm telling you, he was coming on strong. And he had his eyes riveted on my chest."

"Hey, with that dress you were wearing, even *I* kept staring at your chest." We laughed. But the truth was, this news felt like a slap in the face to Thalia. She had actually been considering leaving her marriage for Etienne! Was the affair just another fling to him? I remembered what Julien had said about his father insisting that the family come along. Maybe Etienne was trying to show Thalia where his priorities lay.

I dropped off the dog at home, then stopped by the shop to pick up the mail, water the plants on the patio, and retrieve any deliveries that the store down the block was holding for me. I was surprised to see a news van parked out in front of Le Jardin. As I approached the front door, keys in hand, a forty-something woman in a blue pantsuit stamped out a cigarette on the sidewalk, rushed over to me, and stuck out her hand. "I'm Barbara Abrams from the *Chronicle*," she said in a raspy voice. "You're Rae Sullivan, aren't you? I'm wondering if I could have a few words with you."

I shook my head and muttered, "Sorry," as I unlocked the door and stepped inside. She was right behind me, holding the door ajar with her foot. "I promise it won't take long," she said. "The media is sensationalizing the hell out of the murder. I want to give readers the human side of the story. Fair and balanced, I always say."

I sighed. "OK. What do you want to know?"

"Great! Rae, we'd like to get a picture of you." She beckoned to her cameraman. Before I could protest, he was flipping on lights and instructing me where to stand. I let him snap a few pictures and then said, "I don't have much time. Can we get to the questions?"

"Sure. Sure," she said, but the photographer continued snapping away, until I finally put my hand up over my face. She told him to wrap it up and wait outside. I invited her to sit with me on the patio. "You don't mind if I record our conversation, do you?" she asked, turning on the tape. "I want to make absolutely sure I get it all down accurately," she said.

It went well at first. I said good things about Thalia, what a dreadful shock it was, et cetera. Then she ambushed me. "This decor is really lovely," she gushed. "But I'm not surprised, given your art background." It appeared she had done her homework. "You used to work at Barnaby & Sloane Auction House, didn't you?"

"That's right."

"According to my research, you left when the big scandal broke—"

I cut her off. "That's ancient history. I'm happy to tell you about Thalia and what a great loss her death is. But my background is completely irrelevant."

"But that's when you opened the shop with Thalia Holcombe, isn't it? No other auction house or art gallery would hire you—"

"We're done here. I'd like you to leave now." I got up and walked to the front door. Reluctantly, she followed, still asking questions. I held the door open for her as she left, then slammed it behind her and turned the lock. The photographer continued to snap pictures of the storefront for a few more minutes before they drove off. What a PR disaster.

My time at Barnaby & Sloane was a chapter in my life I definitely didn't want to revisit. My job had started off so promisingly. Fresh out of grad school with a master's in art history, I was hired as a researcher in the antiquities department. It was challenging work that entailed long hours—and a new, grown-up wardrobe—but I loved it. My boss, Virginia, was a terrific mentor, teaching me the business from the ground up. I not only worked with collectors and dealers from all over the country, but

I also got to rub shoulders with San Francisco's elite patrons of the arts at parties in Pacific Heights.

It was at one of those gatherings that I met Hubert Grebe, a jovial dumpling of a man who I guessed to be in his midforties. Originally from Switzerland, he was an international banking executive now based in the Bay Area. We talked for a bit about his work and then moved on to the auction business. "You know, I've never dealt with an auction house," he said. "But I do have a few things I'd like to sell. I travel quite often, so perhaps it makes sense to have you handle the sale rather than me doing it privately." He peppered me with questions, and I did my best to explain the process to him. "That all sounds very good," he said. "I don't know why I didn't think of this before." By the time he left, we were on a first-name basis. He asked for my card.

A few weeks later, Hubert came in with photos of two large landscape paintings, and I introduced him to the appropriate specialist. After meeting with him, she came by to thank me. "I have an appointment to visit Mr. Grebe's home in Hillsborough next week," she said. "I think he's going to turn out to be a high-value customer. Apparently, he has quite a few pieces to sell."

Over the next several months, Hubert did in fact consign a handful of paintings, all of which garnered hefty prices. To thank me for bringing him into the fold, Robert Barnaby gave me a generous bonus—well-timed, since Peter and I were about to go on our honeymoon in Guadeloupe. Shortly after I got back, Hubert came in again, this time with three ivory pieces, which fell in my domain. I authenticated them as nineteenth-century carvings from Japan. Once again they sold for a good price. Hubert told my boss how much he liked working with me, which probably played a role in my subsequent promotion to assistant director of antiquities. Life was good.

I hadn't seen Hubert in a while when he reappeared bearing a large parcel. "You're going to love these," he promised, carefully unwrapping two Etruscan artifacts. They were stunning pieces, one a footed chalice, the other a painted plate. He had bought them from a dealer in Switzerland years ago and hated to part with them, he said. But he needed to downsize because his job was transferring him back to Europe.

Virginia was on vacation, but I authenticated the pieces without hesitation. And they fetched a good price. So good, in fact, that the sale received mention in an art journal for setting a new record. That's when everything fell apart. Thanks to the publicity, the merchandise got the attention of the Italian government, who claimed the pieces were stolen antiquities.

An FBI investigation followed, with hours of depositions and a subpoena of our accounting records. Hubert was mortified and insisted that he'd been swindled by an unscrupulous dealer. Still, the local press skewered us all for not having done due diligence. Worse than the press coverage were the online comments from readers. People who knew nothing whatever about the situation didn't hold back from calling us crooks, scammers, and worse. Although friends wrote comments in my defense, Peter finally made me promise to stop reading anything about the whole incident because I was making myself miserable.

The FBI seized the artifacts and eventually repatriated them to Italy. Barnaby & Sloane paid restitution to the two buyers, one of whom was a prominent collector who ended up suing for damages to his reputation. The auction house took out a full-page ad in major newspapers across the country, apologizing and insisting that we did not condone any such fraudulent behavior. But the board of directors was unforgiving. Robert and I were both fired. Virginia came through unscathed and graciously gave me a nice reference. Still, no one would hire me.

That's when Thalia had come to the rescue, taking me on as a partner. About six months later, the auction house, unable to fully recover from the scandal, shut down. Robert retired to Costa Rica. Last I'd heard, Virginia was in Santa Fe, running an art gallery. We didn't keep in touch.

CHAPTER 12

The Porsche inched along the narrow, rain-slicked street in Ross, making its way in a long line of cars to the church parking lot for Thalia's funeral. Contributing to the snarl were two TV news vans parked on the no-parking-allowed side of the street, opposite the church's broad front stairs. At least they had pulled up partway onto the sidewalk to leave some room for traffic to squeeze by. And at least the throng of reporters were staying on their side of the street to shoot video footage rather than shoving microphones into the mourners' faces.

The lot was full by the time we reached it, so Peter dropped me off in front and went to look for street parking. I hurried up the broad steps to Garrett, who was in front of the church's big double doors, shaking hands and receiving hugs as people filed past him. His fair hair was matted against his head from the steady drizzle that was coming down, but he seemed to take no notice. He hugged me and agreed to my offer to stand with him until everyone was inside. I moved under the eaves to stay dry.

A sizable crowd turned out to bid Thalia goodbye—I recognized a few local politicos, Thalia and Garrett's country club friends, and even some of our regular customers from the shop. I spotted Detective Hernandez looking somber in a dark suit and gray tie. A gleaming town car pulled up, and San Francisco Mayor Romero emerged. No doubt, stopping directly in front of the news crew was a calculated move. Several reporters swarmed around Romero. He spoke to them for a few minutes, probably decrying the tragic death of Thalia Holcombe while working in a plug for himself. It was an election year, after all.

A few minutes later, I spotted Etienne's party coming down the block. Renata was hard to miss. She had on a shiny black raincoat, lacy black gloves, and a wide-brimmed hat that sprouted an assemblage of black feathers. Did she always travel with funeral attire handy, I wondered, or had she shopped especially for the occasion? Etienne held an umbrella over both of them, guarding the plumage from the rain. Julien, Marcel, and Jerome followed behind. As they mounted the steps, Etienne gave Hernandez a puzzled look, and then recognition crossed his face and he nodded.

I smiled at Renata, Etienne, and Jerome in turn, hugged Julien, and completely ignored Marcel. A minute later, Peter dashed up the steps and embraced Garrett, who urged us to go inside. "I'll join you in a minute," he said. Peter took my arm and led me into the church.

Soft music was playing as we made our way to our seats in the front. The air was thick with the perfume of the floral arrangements that carpeted the altar and lined the steps. And the coffin was draped with Sally Holmes roses interspersed with forget-me-nots. Thalia had always admired the simplicity of those roses when she saw them in bloom at my house. It took a dozen phone calls to find a florist who could create what I wanted. Peter and I slipped into the front row, where Thalia's mother, Helena, was already seated, looking regal—and dry-eyed—in a gray silk suit. Luc sat next to her. A moment later, Garrett took the aisle seat in our row.

I sat silently, feeling a bit out of my element. Growing up, I'd only gone to church for family weddings or christenings. For the most part, my father happily ignored his Catholic upbringing. My mother, too, had no interest in religious ritual. The only nod to her Jewish heritage was making latkes for Hanukkah. She'd once said to me, "Why do we need ten commandments when two will cover it? Be a good person and work hard." Good advice, Mom.

The music ceased and the murmuring crowd grew quiet as the minister stepped to the podium. The familiar, comforting ritual began—reading Bible verses, singing hymns, issuing prayers. The minister spoke warmly of Thalia's charity work, her zest for life, and her devotion to her husband—ouch.

"Thalia's brother would now like to say a few words," the minister announced. Luc went up to the podium. He looked pale and worn but was smartly dressed in a navy blue suit and sky blue tie. "My sister was my inspiration," he said quietly. "When I thought of leaving Chicago to buy a farm in France, I asked her what she thought. She answered without hesitation. 'You must do it, of course,' she said. 'You never know how much time you have left. It's a sin to waste a moment.'"

As I fumbled for a tissue, Peter reached into his pocket for a handkerchief, which he pressed into my palm. Luc went on. "I can say that my sister is one of the few people I've met who never wasted a moment. Her charity work, her business with her lifelong friend"—here he looked up at me and smiled warmly— "her exceptional dinner parties. She put herself fully into everything she did. And had she known her life was soon to end, I'm sure she would have arranged her own funeral just to be sure it was all orchestrated to perfection."

My turn came next. "Thalia was a true friend," I began,

my voice breaking. I paused and swallowed hard. "Thalia was a true friend," I began again. "She taught me to take chances, to not care what other people thought, and to be myself. Because Thalia was always very much herself. Comfortable in her own skin, confident. She brought incredible focus and passion to everything she did, whether it was learning to sail or making hollandaise sauce." I went on to talk about how she took me on as a business partner when I had a career setback. "Yes, she could be opinionated," I said with a smile. "And yes, she was often brutally honest. But it always came from a place of wanting the best for everyone she touched. Although I'll miss her for the rest of my life, I take comfort in believing that she left this life without a single regret about anything left undone. Au revoir, Thalia."

I returned to my seat, now openly weeping. Peter put his arm around me. "Very well done, love," he whispered, kissing the top of my head.

When the services ended, I told Peter I'd meet him outside, and I headed toward the restroom. Lots of women had the same idea, as the line was snaking out the door and into the vestibule. I saw Renata ahead of me in line but said nothing. When I emerged from a stall, she was standing at the bank of sinks, reapplying her lipstick in front of the mirror. I smiled as I took a spot at the sink next to her. She gave me a smile back. Or at least her mouth briefly curled up, then snapped back. "I won't be going to the grave site," she said.

"Oh?"

"I've arranged to visit an acquaintance in Kentfield while I wait. My husband will pick me up when the formalities for his paramour are finished."

I wasn't sure how to respond, but Renata immediately

continued in a rush of words. "The truth is, I had no fondness for Thalia, and I feel no sadness at her death. So why should I be forced to pretend?" She zipped up her makeup bag and shoved it into her handbag. Turning to face me, she said, "Please don't pity me. My husband was *not* about to leave his family, despite what Thalia may have believed. In fact, he brought us along to show her that we are more important to him than she ever would be."

Then she composed herself and put a hand on my arm. "I mean no disrespect to you. I know she was your friend."

I nodded.

"I just want you to understand. My husband and son come first."

"Of course," I murmured. "You have a very charming son," I added. "I enjoyed my time with him."

"Thank you." This time she smiled for real, then said goodbye.

Outside, reporters converged on Garrett, who waved them away and ducked into the waiting black car. Peter and I drove to the cemetery, a journey made interminably slow by the rain. At last we entered the cemetery gates and drove through the green field to the grave site. Standing in the drizzle, I linked my arm through Sonia's while the reverend spoke. As the pallbearers slowly carried the flower-draped coffin to the grave, I stared into the hole in the ground. This wasn't possible. Surely the coffin held someone else, some anonymous person I had never met. The reverend said a few more words, the coffin was lowered, and Thalia was gone. I stood at the graveside feeling numb.

I looked up to find Marcel watching me. I glared at him, and he lowered his gaze. The minister was inviting the mourners to Garrett's house for refreshments, and people began filing to their cars.

Back in Ross, I watched with approval as the caterer brought out another tray of hot crab cakes from the kitchen and set it on a trivet. Thalia never set hot dishes directly on the sideboard. People were talking quietly as they ate and drank. The mood was less tearful now, almost like a subdued cocktail party—but without the hostess. I remembered Thalia, radiant in her luminous dress, in this same dining room a week ago. How was it possible she was dead?

I offered my condolences to Helena, who accepted a hug without providing one in return. "Luc gave a lovely eulogy," I said.

She smiled wryly. "Yes, it's very gratifying that my children appear to have patched things up after that falling out they had years ago."

"Oh?" I hoped she'd elaborate, but she didn't.

"Ah, well, that's all in the past now," she said. "You look lovely, dear. Much better than that dreadful photograph of you in this morning's newspaper." She smiled sweetly.

They'd probably chosen the most unflattering photo of the lot. Peter had read the *Chronicle* this morning but hadn't let me look at the paper. "Don't stress out over these idiots," he said. "People are commenting just to stir up trouble. Of course you had nothing to do with Thalia's death." Shit. They were sensationalizing the murder, with me as the star villain.

I promised myself that I'd talk to Detective Hernandez again on Monday morning. This emphasis on me as a suspect was ridiculous. I needed to convince him that the blackmail threat was real. Too bad the notes hadn't turned up. Maybe the police hadn't searched thoroughly enough. I was pretty certain Thalia wouldn't have thrown them away. The urge to look through her papers took hold.

Excusing myself, I went upstairs to her study, locking the door behind me. I sat in her silk-upholstered chair and slid open the top drawer of the desk. Empty. I opened each of the side drawers. Also empty. Had the murderer been in Thalia's office, covering his tracks? Then I realized the police had probably taken everything, which I found reassuring. Maybe they hadn't completely dismissed the possibility of blackmail. Maybe they'd find the notes.

I closed the drawers and pushed the chair back in. As I stepped out into the hall and shut the door quietly behind me, a voice said, "What were you doing in there?" I jumped. It was Peter. "Are you all right? I saw you go upstairs a while ago."

"Yes, I'm fine. I just wanted to go into Thalia's office."

"Why?" he asked.

"I . . . I just wanted to sit there and think about her." I knew Peter didn't approve of my sleuthing.

He gave me a hug and said, "I want to apologize for all the times I complained about Thalia. I know she meant a lot to you. I'm sorry she's gone."

We went downstairs and saw that people were beginning to leave. "Peter, I'm going to stay and help clean up. Why don't you go home and come back for me later."

"Are you sure you're up to that?" he asked, stroking my cheek. "You look exhausted."

"Yes, I'll actually feel better to be doing something useful."

"OK. Do you want me to stay here with you?"

"No, no. I'll be fine."

I began clearing the buffet table. Sonia came over, raincoat in hand. "How are you holding up?" she asked me.

"I'm OK. I just need to grab some food," I said, snatching a crab cake from the platter. "I'm going to stay a few more hours and help clean up. I don't want Garrett to be alone. Luc has moved to a hotel with his mother."

"Are you all right? Want me to keep you company?"

"No, I'm fine. Really."

Luc came over to say goodbye. "Are you OK?" he asked, holding on to my shoulders and looking at me with concern.

I smiled. "You're the third person to ask me that in the last five minutes. I'm fine." I'm fine, I silently repeated. I'd made it through the funeral. On Monday I'd have a long talk with Detective Hernandez. It would all get straightened out.

"I'm flying out tomorrow night," he told me. "It was wonderful to see you. You'll come for a visit, won't you? I can't leave unless you agree."

I promised I would and hugged him goodbye, the loss of Thalia somehow magnified by Luc's departure.

CHAPTER 13

It was eight in the evening by the time I had put away three dishwasher loads of clean plates, stowed the leftovers in the fridge, and stacked all the caterer's paraphernalia to be picked up the following day. I was longing to go home, but Garrett had asked me to do one more thing: to look through Thalia's closet and take anything I wanted before Helena boxed it all up for donation tomorrow. Reluctantly, I trudged upstairs.

I walked into the darkened bedroom, my feet sinking into the plush carpet. As I fumbled for the switch on a bedside lamp, a voice from across the room said, "I loved her, you know."

"Oh, God, you scared me." I turned the light on, revealing Garrett seated on a settee opposite the bed, a glass of scotch in one hand and a nearly empty bottle in the other. He murmured an apology. He was clearly drunk and looked absolutely miserable.

I offered to come back in the morning to go through Thalia's clothes, but he insisted that he welcomed the company. "She was something," he said, shaking his head. "I can't believe she's gone. Rae, to tell you the truth, I'm not sure I can keep going without her. She took care of me. She had my shirts ironed. Hell, she bought my shirts. I never knew what looked right."

I had been struggling with similar doubts of my own. Sure, Thalia exasperated me at times—a lot of times. But she was my rock. No matter what happened, I knew she'd be there for me. And now . . . well, I needed to be my own rock. "Garrett, you'll be fine. It will get easier. Not right away, but it will." I hoped the words didn't sound as trite to him as they did to me.

Not knowing what else to say, I decided to take a quick look through Thalia's clothes and go home. As I opened the louvered doors of her enormous walk-in closet, a faint trace of her scent wafted out. "Have the police gone through all this?" I asked.

"Dunno. They emptied her nightstand drawers, but they spent most of their time in her office. Boxed up all her personal papers."

I wasn't expecting to find anything I wanted among Thalia's clothes. Although everything was lovely, it just wasn't my style—lots of pale hues and silky fabrics that suited her well but didn't appeal to me. I wasn't a pastels kind of gal. Idly, I tried on a few pairs of her elegant shoes, but they were too big. The charity shop would certainly be pleased with this sizable haul of designer couture.

Two boxes on the top shelf caught my eye. I hauled one down and brought it to the bed, quickly becoming absorbed in its trove of photos from years past: birthday parties, summer vacations, a young Thalia and Luc opening Christmas presents. I wondered whether it had been hard for Luc when Thalia and her mother came into his life. His father had married Helena mere months after his first wife died. And Helena certainly wasn't the warmest person in the world. "My mother never hugged me because it creased her blouse," Thalia once told me ruefully. Not exactly what a recently bereaved boy wants in a stepmother.

What a contrast to my own mother, who welcomed every

neighborhood kid into our Brooklyn apartment, no matter how much mess they created—or how much food they devoured. I smiled at the memory. Even now, my mother worried about me. She'd been calling daily since the murder, making sure I was OK and offering to fly out to help.

"I'm going to offer a reward," Garrett said, interrupting my thoughts. "Ten thousand dollars. Maybe then the dickhead police will finally get the right person." He swallowed more scotch. "They think it's me, you know. Because Thalia was having an affair." He was mostly talking to himself and didn't seem to mind that I offered no response.

I fetched the second box and returned to the bed. More photos, which I didn't linger over, some old letters, and, beneath those, a pair of tiny white gloves wrapped in tissue. They must have been Thalia's once upon a time, judging from the way her mother dressed her in the photos. I decided to stash these boxes in Thalia's office so that Helena didn't send them off to the thrift store. I took the first box down the hall. When I returned to the bedroom, Garrett was standing by the bed, staring at the little white gloves.

"She was saving these," he said, "hoping that someday we'd have a daughter."

I was speechless. Thalia had wanted kids? That was something she'd never mentioned to me.

Garrett took a gulp of Scotch and began pacing the room. "We had been trying for a year to have a baby. But I wasn't worried. It's something we thought we had time for." He laughed humorlessly. "Of course, it didn't work out the way I thought."

"No," I said with sympathy.

"She was pregnant. That's what the police told me."

I froze. "What?"

His eyes narrowed. "You don't have to pretend." His lips curled upward, but it was more a baring of teeth than a smile. "Yes, Thalia got knocked up by her French lover. How's that for a kick in the face?"

"What are you talking about?"

"Don't bullshit me, Rae," he growled. "You must have known. You were her closest friend." He glared at me with a murderous look on his face. "Of course, she couldn't be bothered to tell me. I'm only her damn husband."

I swallowed. "Garrett, what are you talking about?"

"Did everyone know but me?" he said plaintively, resuming his pacing. "It's bad enough that she was screwing that Frenchman, but pregnant? Pregnant? Four weeks. Do the fucking math," he shouted. He came over to me, his face looming inches from mine. The alcohol scent was overpowering. "You knew," he said accusingly, jabbing his finger into my chest. "She told everyone but me."

I swallowed. "No, of course not. I had no idea." I was pierced by grief—for Thalia's lost baby, for Garrett, and for myself. How much worse could this get? I wanted to flee, to be alone and process this bombshell.

"How stupid I was!" Again his voice rose. "Did everyone know but me? That pansy-ass Frenchman, her brother, everyone. And I had to find out from the goddamn police!" He was shouting even louder now.

"Garrett—"

"No, don't you dare say a word." He raised his palm toward me, and I winced, fearing he was going to strike me, but he spun around toward the settee again and almost lost his balance. "I'm tired of everyone's sympathy. She played me for a fool!" He sat down with a thump and drained his glass. "She played me for a fool!"

Thankfully, my phone rang. It was Peter, calling to see if I was ready to be picked up. "Yeah, I'm just finishing," I told him, my voice shaky. "Come get me. Right now."

Garrett put his head in his hands. "Oh, God, Rae, I'm sorry. It's all too much." He began to sob.

"We both need to get some sleep," I said. "I'll be done here in a minute." I closed up the second box and carried it into Thalia's office, then came back and said good night, giving the closet one last look. Maybe I should take something after all, I thought, something to hold on to. I spotted Thalia's gray blazer. It was the jacket she'd worn when we met at the farmers market, the day I'd stormed off in a huff. "Garrett, would it be OK if I take this?"

"Of course."

I took it off the hanger and went through the pockets, emptying out the spare change onto the nightstand. And there it was in the inside breast pocket. Before I even unfolded it, I knew what it was. I stared at the note demanding money.

"What's that?" Garrett asked.

Without a word, I handed it to him.

He stood looking down at the page for a long time—much longer than it could have taken to read the few sentences. Was he, too, feeling that the person he thought he'd known was an utter stranger?

Finally, he sat down on the bed, looking miserable. "I . . . I guess the police need to see this."

I took the note gently from his hand. "I'll bring it to them on Monday," I promised.

CHAPTER 14

On Monday morning I marched into Park Police Station at one minute to eleven. "I have an appointment with Detective Hernandez," I said to the officer at the desk, this time a woman. Hernandez came out and led me into that same sparse room with the scuffed table and the uncomfortable chairs. Warren was there. I extracted the letter from my purse and handed it to Hernandez, feeling quite proud of myself. "I found this in Thalia's jacket." I refrained from making a snide comment about their failure to search thoroughly.

Hernandez put on a pair of latex gloves before reaching for it. He read it slowly, then passed it to Warren, who also donned gloves and scanned it more quickly. Then Hernandez sealed the note in an evidence bag and labeled it. "Tell me where you found this," he said.

"I was going through Thalia's things. It was in the pocket of one of her jackets."

"And you're sure this is the note you saw earlier?"

I insisted that it was the same one I had seen at the farmers market. "You'll test it for fingerprints, won't you?" I asked.

Hernandez assured me they would but wanted to know who else had handled it.

"Just me and Garrett," I said. "He was there when I found it." They gave each other a meaningful glance. "Oh, and my husband," I added. "I showed it to him when I got home. That's all."

"That's all?" Warren asked facetiously. I realized I should have been more careful. What if someone had smudged Marcel's fingerprints? "Sorry," I said contritely. "I handled it before I realized what it was."

"And how about after you realized?" Warren inquired. I didn't have a good answer to that. Hernandez said quickly, "Thank you for bringing this in. We'll send this off to forensics right away. We'll need to take your fingerprints so we can eliminate them. And we'll need your husband to come in, as well. But first we have some additional questions for you."

"Of course. I'm happy to help."

"It's about the life insurance payment."

I waited. Presumably he had a question.

"According to the documents, you'll personally be getting half a million dollars."

"No, that can't be right," I said with a laugh. "The business wasn't worth that much—"

"It's based on earnings over the next twenty years. With the loss of either partner, the business would be in serious difficulty."

"Yes, but—"

Hernandez held up a hand. "Mrs. Sullivan, what you think is reasonable is not the issue here. The fact is that you are about to be paid a sizable settlement."

Warren jumped in. "I'm sure your husband will be pleased."

"Well, yes . . . of course. But no! He wouldn't want Thalia to die just so we could collect the insurance! What are you saying?"

"What we're saying is actually pretty simple," Warren said, leaning across the table. "Your husband is in a financial bind.

A big one. He has some pretty unsavory characters that he owes money to. Being in hock to loan sharks is dangerous business."

His self-satisfied expression made me want to hit him. "That's not true!" I protested. "You're making that up. He's had some real estate losses, but nothing we can't handle. Are you accusing him of killing Thalia?"

"No. Not directly. His alibi is airtight." He consulted his notes. "He was at that architect event from seven thirty on, and Thalia called you at 8:22. Your husband didn't leave until around ten, except for a quick break when he phoned you. And you're apparently in the clear too, since you had a dinner guest. But you see, when this much money is involved, well, it makes us wonder."

This was incredible. Did they seriously think that Peter and I had plotted Thalia's murder? I stared at them, Warren looking smug, Hernandez's face showing concern. They weren't kidding. "By your own admission," Warren said, "you knew that Mrs. Holcombe would be a sitting duck alone in the park. In fact, according to you, you're the only one who knew." I was about to ask for a lawyer but stopped myself. First off, I didn't have a lawyer—other than Garrett. Second, on TV the blustery suspect who demands a lawyer is invariably guilty, and I didn't want to give the wrong impression.

Instead, I decided it was time to leave. "Your allegations are ridiculous. I have another appointment. Can I go now?"

"Not quite yet," said Hernandez. He opened another folder and scanned some papers. "Tell me about your work at Barnaby & Sloane."

First the reporter, now the police. "What about it?" I asked. "I was the associate director of the collectibles department. I worked there for three and a half years."

Warren said, "Yeah, until the company was caught selling

stolen antiquities. The CEO is lucky he's not serving time. And so are you. You authenticated the merchandise."

"Yes. Yes, I did. But it *was* authentic. That was never in dispute."

"Authentic but stolen." Warren leaned in close to me as he said the last word. "We've been talking to some of your former colleagues. They say that you were Robert Barnaby's protégé. He brought you in, groomed you, and promoted you after only two months."

"What's your point?" I asked, struggling to maintain my composure.

"My point is that if you were such a superstar, how did you screw up so badly? By the way, some of your former coworkers don't like you very much. They blame you for bringing down the company and costing them their jobs. The way I see it, it's entirely possible you and Barnaby and that Swiss guy were in on this little scam together." I started to protest, but Warren cut me off. "Sure, I know no charges were filed, but lack of proof isn't the same as innocence." He gave Hernandez a wink. "We've seen that happen more times than we can count."

Warren still wasn't done. "Then the company was sued by the purchaser of the urn. Tell us, what was the result of that suit?"

"I'm pretty sure you already know," I said angrily. "The auction house was found liable and had to repay the buyer, plus one hundred thousand in damages. And of course the artifacts were returned to Italy."

"And that was the end of Barnaby & Sloane, wasn't it? Not to mention that your own reputation was ruined too. No one would hire you at an auction house or art gallery after that little incident, would they?" I said nothing. "You were not trustworthy."

"What happened had nothing to do with my honesty! I told you, my boss was away and there was no one to research the provenance. We trusted Hubert Grebe because we'd worked with him before."

Warren wasn't interested in my explanation. "That's when your pal Thalia Holcombe bailed you out. She took you on as a partner. But my guess is you resented her—"

"Bullshit!" I wasn't going to listen to any more of this. I pushed back my chair and stood up. "If that's all, I'm leaving."

"You can go. But make sure you don't leave the Bay Area," Warren warned me. "We've got our eye on you. Oh, and don't expect that insurance money anytime soon. Until we give them the go-ahead, they're not paying you a dime."

CHAPTER 15

The early rains had caused oxalis to sprout everywhere among the flowers and veggies. As I knelt in the dirt and pulled out the intruders, I felt myself relaxing. I scooped up my pickings and dumped them into the compost pile. I gave the pile a few turns with a pitchfork, happy to see a bevy of earthworms hard at work. Bees were buzzing in the salvia, two hummingbirds were dipping their long beaks into the California fuchsia, and Jasper was lolling in the sunshine.

Unbidden, the scene of Thalia's death came into my mind. Her body lying in the mud, surrounded by human detritus: the soiled sleeping bags, empty beer bottles, McDonald's wrappers, a discarded Louis Vuitton shopping bag filled with filthy clothes. A scattering of cigarette butts.

I went inside and phoned Hernandez. "This is Rae Sullivan," I told him. "I understand from Garrett that you think Thalia told him she was pregnant and that it was a motive for him to kill her. Well, that can't be true."

"Hello, Mrs. Sullivan. What makes you say that Mrs. Holcombe didn't tell her husband about her pregnancy?"

"It's obvious," I said, feeling proud of my deductive reasoning. "She was smoking on the night she was killed. I saw her cigarette butts near her body. Gauloises. She would never have smoked if she'd known she was pregnant. Never!"

He was silent for a moment. Then he said, "We were aware the cigarettes were the victim's. Your insight into her likely behavior is helpful. But, of course, the cigarettes don't prove that she was unaware of the pregnancy. Perhaps she had decided to terminate it."

I didn't know what to say. He was right. That was certainly a possibility. "Oh. Yes. Well, I just thought you should know," I finished lamely.

"Nonetheless, I appreciate your help. Please call if you think of anything else."

"I will." I hung up, feeling foolish. Of course Thalia might not want to have a child with Etienne. All sorts of possibilities were occurring to me. What if Etienne knew about the pregnancy and didn't want Thalia to have an abortion? Would he have become violent? No, that made no sense. If he wanted the child, he wouldn't kill Thalia. Or what if he was the one wanting to end the pregnancy, and she was determined to have the baby? But if that were true, I was sure she wouldn't have been smoking. In either case, why would Etienne try to extort money?

It all came back to those blackmail notes. Unless . . . I stood in the kitchen lost in thought. What if the note was a sham, only intended to lure Thalia to a dark, lonely spot? Suppose the "blackmailer" was lying in wait, intending to kill her all along.

But why the first note? There was no plausible explanation. Perhaps it really *was* a mugging—a case of Thalia being in the wrong place at the wrong time. Still, whoever had lured her to the park with that note bore some responsibility for her death. I was determined to uncover who it was.

I heard Peter's car pull into the driveway. Time for a talk. I didn't want to start a fight, but I had to know what was going on with our finances. A minute later, he came in through the back door. "Hi, love," he said, giving me a kiss. "Your face is smudged with dirt, you know." He took out a handkerchief and dabbed at my forehead.

"Peter, we need to talk."

"What's wrong?" he asked.

"Nothing, I hope. But the police told me some things that really upset me today, and I need to ask you about them."

"OK, I have to make a few phone calls. Let's talk over dinner."

I had some business emails to take care of, anyway. I busied myself with that until dinner was ready, then called Peter. He came downstairs, grabbed a beer from the fridge, and said, "I'm all ears."

I sat down across from him. "Peter, the police said you owe a lot of money. Is it true?"

"Well, yes, I'm in a bit of a hole, but it's nothing serious. I've been there before. As I keep telling you, love, you've got to take some risks if you want to make money." He heaped potatoes, salad, and slices of roast beef onto his plate. "This looks delicious."

"But, Peter, they said you've been borrowing from loan sharks."

He laughed. "Private sources, darling, private sources. That doesn't make them loan sharks. Look, there's nothing for you to worry about. And why were the police even interested?"

"Because they think you and I plotted to kill Thalia for the insurance money."

He burst out laughing. "You and I? Look, I won't deny that the money is coming at a very good time. In fact, I recently borrowed some funds from a friend. But the thought of you plotting to kill anyone is laughable. You won't even swat a spider. The police are just trying to rattle you."

"Why would they do that?"

He shrugged. "Maybe because they have no leads." He drank some more of his beer. "But you know, this is a good time to tell you something I've been thinking about." He paused. "How would you feel about moving to Arizona?"

I must have had a less-than-overjoyed look on my face because he immediately said, "Just for a while. Not permanently." He went on to explain. The real estate market had tanked. Houses were sitting empty. We'd rent out our Fairfax home and go live in one of the vacant properties. He'd renovate it—"cheaply, of course. No more than the market will bear"—and sell it. Then move to the next house. "You'll do the landscaping, I'll do the remodeling, and then we'll flip them," Peter said. "The timing is perfect. The market is heating up again, and I can recoup my losses." He reached out and took hold of my hand. "This is a great opportunity for us, Rae."

"So you'd give up your business?" I asked.

"No, no. I'd fly back every few weeks to meet with clients. I can do the designing from Arizona. My crew here can totally handle the construction without me breathing down their necks. My foreman is top-notch."

"But what about the shop?" I asked.

"What about it? You've often said it was all Thalia's idea, anyway. Here's your chance to do more landscape design. And we'd get to work together." He was clearly excited. "We both need a change. This will be good for you . . . for us."

With Thalia's murder, I didn't think I could stand any more change in my life at the moment, but Peter was so enthusiastic that I wanted to be supportive. I nodded (convincingly, I hoped). "Let me think about it. It could be fun."

"Of course it will be fun. You think about it and let's talk again tomorrow."

I smiled and nodded. Tomorrow? How soon was he planning this move?

Later that evening, as Peter watched TV, I thought for a long time about Le Jardin. True, it had never been my idea. It was Thalia's way of rescuing me from a bad situation. She'd just opened the shop when everything at the auction house blew up, and she generously invited me to go into business with her. I was grateful for the opportunity, no doubt about it. And as it turned out, I was good at it. Better than I'd ever dreamed. The shop was thriving. Damn it, I didn't want to give up the business that Thalia and I had worked so hard to build. At least not for Arizona.

CHAPTER 16

The next morning, I stood in front of 275 Grant Avenue, a narrow three-story building in the heart of Chinatown. This was the address I'd found in Marcel's hotel room. The street was jammed with people—locals doing their grocery shopping and tourists hitting the trinket shops. I stepped from the brightness of the day into a small, dark lobby. Unsure where to go next, I peered at a panel that listed all the businesses in the building. Crap! It was in Chinese. I was going to have to try them all. At least there were only four floors and only two businesses listed per floor. I pressed the "up" arrow to summon the elevator, but its creaks and groans didn't inspire confidence. I opted for the stairs.

My first try hit an impasse. I didn't blame the woman who sat at the reception desk. Since I couldn't utter a word in her language, it was no surprise that she was unaccommodating. I showed her a picture of Marcel on my phone, which I'd asked Julien to send me. She shook her head dismissively, and I left. I fared slightly better at the other company on that floor, which appeared to be some sort of clothing factory. Behind the entryway was a huge room, full of women busy at sewing machines. Here, the manager spoke English, and I felt less foolish. But he, too, denied recognizing Marcel.

The next floor up yielded the same non-results. On I trudged, with a newfound respect for professional detectives. It was becoming apparent that you hit a lot of dead ends before you found out something useful.

On the fourth floor, I knocked at the first door and received a reply in a language I didn't understand but that sounded welcoming. I opened the door. The large, sky-lighted room was outfitted floor to ceiling with shelves, all crammed with jars. Some looked like tea leaves or other herbs; others held more dubious contents floating in liquid.

"Hello," I said tentatively.

"Hello, hello." A small Asian man smiled at me. "I am Dr. Lee. How can I help you?"

I showed him the photo of Marcel. "Do you recognize this man?" I asked.

He nodded. "Yes, yes, very nice man. I was able to help him."

I tried not to look as clueless as I felt. "Great," I said. "Er, can you tell me what he wanted?"

The man laughed. "You're not his girlfriend, are you?"

"Oh, no! No!"

He laughed harder. "I didn't think so. A beautiful lady like you, he wouldn't need help from me." He winked.

It took me a moment, but it finally dawned on me what he was talking about. Marcel had come for some sort of herbal Viagra.

"I sold him tiger penis. Guaranteed to help with the ladies."

"Tiger penis? Is it really from tigers?" I was horrified.

His smile faded. "How come you ask about that?" He looked mistrustful. "Are you police?"

"No, no," I assured him. "My friend was very happy with what you sold him. That's why he told me to come here for my high blood pressure."

He remained unconvinced. "Then why do you show me his picture?"

It was apparent that my cover story left a lot to be desired. "I just wanted to make sure I was in the right place," I said, hoping that sounded plausible. "His handwriting was hard to read."

That satisfied Dr. Lee, and his engaging grin returned. "It would be my pleasure to help you." He took down one of the jars with what looked like an octopus floating in it. "Mrs. Wong's placenta," he said. "You steep a piece in boiling water. Make tea. Very good for you." Trying not to gag, I purchased what I sincerely hoped was not an actual placenta. Dr. Lee gave me some dietary advice for my fictional medical condition, which I promised to follow.

"Oh, do you remember what day my friend was here?" I asked casually. Now that we were buddies, he apparently didn't find this question suspicious. He checked his stack of sales slips, which were skewered on a spindle.

"Here it is. One ounce dried tiger penis. September one." The night Thalia was killed.

"What time do you close?" I asked.

"Five o'clock."

So Marcel would certainly have had enough time to get to Golden Gate Park at six thirty to pick up the money. But then why was he late? Why hadn't Thalia confronted him until after eight o'clock? I needed to find out where he went after Chinatown so I could reconstruct the events of that evening. But as I expected, Dr. Lee didn't know anything about where Marcel had been going next. I thanked him and left.

I was ten minutes late for my lunch date with Sonia a few blocks away. When I joined her at a table, she already had three small plates in front of her. "Hope you don't mind that I started without you," she said between mouthfuls of shrimp dumplings. She flagged down the waiter rolling the dim sum cart and pointed to a plate of steamed pork buns, her armful of silver bracelets jangling. "We'll take some of those too."

"My visit to Grant Avenue was interesting," I said. "It's an herb shop run by a man named Dr. Lee. His shop is full of weird crap in jars. And Marcel was there all right. Buying tiger penis. Want to guess what it's used for?"

"Migraines?"

"Impotence."

"You're kidding."

"Nope. He was there the night of the murder. But he left by five. So he still had time to get to the park. You know, I think it's really from tigers. They kill them to make this stuff. Pathetic. Maybe I should let Hernandez know what's going on."

"Good idea. What's in the bag?"

I hesitated to tell her, since she was still eating with gusto. I waited until she swallowed.

"Mrs. Wong's placenta."

"Holy shit. Human organ trafficking?"

"I doubt it, unless Mrs. Wong gives birth every fifteen minutes. He had about thirty jars full of the stuff. You make a tea out of it for high blood pressure."

"Live and learn," Sonia said. "Here, try this squid roll."

I declined.

CHAPTER 17

Jasper and a shaggy poodle were splashing in a puddle at the dog park, while I sat on a bench lost in thought. Had it only been a week since Thalia was killed? It felt like a lifetime.

I thought of Thalia's first call to me as she walked toward Golden Gate Park. And then again a little later from Smitty's. She had been so excited about her plan to catch Marcel. Why hadn't I talked her out of it? Or why hadn't she taken Luc with her like I'd asked her to? I was sure now that she'd intended the whole time to go back into Golden Gate Park and confront him. The bus backup just made it easier.

Suddenly, I remembered. She had seen something—or someone. What had she said? "Son of a bitch." No, "That son of a bitch." So definitely someone. But who? She'd insisted it wasn't Marcel and that it had nothing at all to do with the blackmail.

Still, it could be important. How could I have forgotten to tell the police about that? I dialed Hernandez's cell phone. He answered on the second ring. "It's Rae Sullivan," I said.

"What can I do for you?"

"I just remembered something else that Thalia said when she called from Smitty's."

"Yes?"

"She was telling me about going back into the park. And of course I was telling her not to. And then she stopped and said, "That son of a bitch.""

"And then?"

"Um, that's all. She said it was nothing. I thought she'd seen Marcel but she said no, it had nothing to do with him. That's all. I know it doesn't sound like much, but . . ."

"No, everything is important. I appreciate your calling."

"You've talked to the people at Smitty's, right?"

"Yes, certainly," Hernandez said.

"Well maybe you'll want to go back and talk to them again about this. Maybe you can find out what she saw that was so surprising."

"Thank you, Mrs. Sullivan," he said politely. I wondered if he'd do anything with this new information. Screw it. I would go to Smitty's myself.

I waited until early evening, hoping I'd run into some of the same people that had been there last Monday. I showered, changed into black slacks and a fluffy white sweater, and then texted Peter that I would be gone for a few hours and drove into the city to Smitty's. The place was pretty full, with a noise level that was close to a roar. To the left of the door was a long, sleek counter with barstools that ran along the front window. Every stool was occupied. Behind that were about a dozen tables. Along the right wall was the bar, where a stocky man was busy serving a crowd and joking with customers. I found a seat at the end of the bar. It took a minute for the bartender to work his way down to me.

"What can I get you?"

I ordered a Heineken, which the man sitting to my left immediately offered to pay for. "No, thanks," I said with a smile. "I'm actually here on business."

"I like business," he said, sounding as though he'd already had more than one of whatever he was drinking.

Ignoring him, I spoke to the bartender, who was pouring my beer into a chilled glass. "I'm Rae." He introduced himself as Brad. "Brad, were you working last Monday, the night of the murder in the park?" I asked.

"Yep. Matter of fact, I served that beautiful lady. Vodka martini with a twist."

"You have a good memory," I said, impressed. "I'm trying to get some information about someone who may have been following her."

"You a detective?" he asked.

"You could say that." I flashed him a conspiratorial smile. "Did you notice this man here?" I showed him the photo of Marcel.

"Oh, that homely dude. The police already showed me his photo. I've never seen him in here." A customer sitting in the middle of the bar waved to Brad for a refill. "I'll be back," he said.

As soon as Brad stepped away, the guy next to me tried again to make conversation. "So you're a detective. Do you carry a gun?"

"No."

"You sure I can't buy you a drink?"

"Maybe some other time," I told him. A minute later Brad returned. "I know you're busy," I said. "I'm just wondering if anything strange happened while Thalia was here. Did she have a confrontation with anyone?"

"Not that I saw. Like I said, she ordered a martini. She was talking on her phone to someone, real quiet-like. And watching the front windows like she was waiting for someone." That made sense. She was waiting for the buses to pull away so she could make her move. "I served some other customers," Brad continued. "When I came back, she had left. Barely touched her drink. She was a good tipper, though."

"So nothing unusual happened? No disturbance or anything?"

He frowned. "What do you mean?"

"I don't know exactly," I admitted. "But I was the one on the phone with her, and she saw something that surprised her. I was just wondering what it was."

"Sorry, Rae, can't help you with that. The place was jumping. But like I said, she kept watching the window the whole time." Another customer waved to him for a refill. I thanked him and left a big tip—probably not as big as Thalia had left, but sizable.

"Brenda," said the man sitting next to me.

"Excuse me?"

"You should talk to Brenda. She was working on Monday. Ask her if anything happened over there." He nodded toward the counter and the stools along the front window.

"Um, OK, thanks."

I took my glass of beer and intercepted Brenda on her way to place an order. She didn't appreciate being waylaid, but when I told her I was a friend of the murdered woman, she took an interest. She spent a few seconds looking at Marcel's photo, then shook her head.

I posed my question about what Thalia might have seen. "Hmm. I don't remember anything," Brenda replied.

"Ok, thanks." Dead end.

"You know," she said, "you should talk to those guys." She nodded at two fellows over by the pool table. "They come in almost every day after work. Maybe they saw something. I didn't tell the police to talk to them. Them being here illegally and all. But you seem nice enough."

"OK, thanks for your help." Still clutching my beer, I moseyed over to the pool table.

"Hi," I said, not sure how to break the ice. The two of them looked at me with interest. One had flaming red hair and a red beard. The other was dark-haired and wore a tweed cap.

"Good evening," said the red-haired fellow in a thick Irish brogue.

"Brenda said you might be able to help me." I explained that I was a friend of the murdered woman and was trying to get some information.

"That lady who was killed in the park?" asked the one in the cap.

"That's right. I understand you're in here most nights. Did either of you see her last Monday?" I showed Thalia's photo. Neither recalled having seen her, although they recognized her face from the news coverage. Next I showed them Marcel's photo. Nothing.

"OK. One more question. Did anything unusual happen while you were here?"

They both shrugged at each other. "No, just the usual."

"No fights, no incidents? Anything at all out of the ordinary?"

"No," said the redhead. But then he turned toward his pal, saying, "Wait, hold on. There was that one girl, the one who you bought a beer."

"Tell me about her," I said to the other man.

"She said some bloke had been chatting her up and got up to go to the john. Real sudden. Then she saw him come out of the john and dash out the door. She was plenty ticked off."

"What did the man look like?"

"I never saw him. She came over to our table after he was gone. She was pretty drunk by then."

"Have you seen her in here again?"

Neither of them had. "Well, if you do, could you ask her to call me? Here's my card. Even better, try to get her phone number for me. That should be easy for two handsome fellows like you."

"There's a reward, right?"

"Yes, if your information leads to catching the murderer, there's a big reward. You and this girl could split it. So make sure you call me." They promised they would.

CHAPTER 18

I reopened for business the next day. Dozens of people from the neighboring shops on San Anselmo Avenue stopped by to offer condolences. Some brought flowers. The owner of the bagel store sent a huge tray of food, which I set out for customers.

Good thing I had arranged for Susan to switch to full time. The high-profile case with glamorous Thalia plastered all over the front pages proved to be a big draw. Who knew murder would be so good for business? In fact, it was probably boosting traffic for the whole street, since many people confessed they had never been to (or even heard of) San Anselmo before. "What a quaint little town," was a common refrain.

Although most customers expressed sympathy, some came in simply to gawk—and offer up theories to one another. I heard whispered suggestions of a political hit, the victim's lesbian lover, and even the Russian mafia.

And then there was a designer-clad pair who appeared to be mother and daughter. "That's her," the older woman said in a loud nasal voice. "From the Barnaby & Sloane scandal. I knew it! It's no wonder she changed her name."

"Can I help you find something?" I asked her.

"Oh, we're just looking," said her younger clone.

"Actually, you're doing more than looking," I said icily. "You're gossiping about me, which I don't appreciate, especially since I just lost a very close friend."

They sputtered a bit, then turned and walked out the door. An elderly lady waiting to pay for her purchase said, "Good for you, dear. Some people just have no manners."

I worked all day without a break, barely having a spare minute to go to the bathroom. When it was finally closing time, I met Sonia around the corner for a taco. We sat at an outside table so that Jasper could lie next to us while we ate.

"Have you met Detective Levine?" Sonia asked.

"No. Who's he?"

"Another detective who's working on the case. Hernandez and Warren were busy, so Levine interviewed me."

"Is he a jerk like Warren?"

"No, not at all. He's nice. And he's cute. Well, not physically cute. He's kind of nerdy looking, and he's losing his hair. But he's funny. And he knows stuff."

"What kind of stuff?"

"Everything. He reads a lot. He asked what kind of work I do, and we talked for a half hour about midcentury modern furniture design."

"So he's gay?"

"Definitely not," Sonia said.

"How do you know?"

"I know," she said with certainty. "He almost asked me out. But of course he can't while he's working on the case. Once it's over, maybe."

I couldn't picture Sonia with a balding police officer. Her boyfriends were typically struggling artists and musicians. Someone with a steady paycheck would be a new experience for her.

"By the way," she said, "this salsa is almost as good as my grandma's secret recipe. Almost. I'll bring you back a jar next time I visit her in LA."

This was as good a time as any to drop my bombshell. "Peter wants to move to Arizona."

Sonia's hand froze over the bowl of chips. "What!"

"Yep. I'm ignoring the whole thing, hoping it will go away. He has property there that he needs to deal with. And he thinks it will be good for me."

"What are you, sixty-five years old? What does he mean, 'good for you'?"

"You know. A change."

"Allow me to remind you that you hate the desert," Sonia said. "You love the ocean. The redwoods. And you don't play golf, which I think is a legal requirement in Arizona," she added snidely.

"So you're saying it's a bad idea."

"Of course. You don't know anyone there. And what about the shop?"

"Oh, I don't know," I mused. "That was always Thalia's thing, really. I'm kind of at loose ends. I have to admit, I *am* feeling like I need a change."

"Dye your hair," she said, scooping up more salsa on a chip.

"Sonia, I'm serious."

"So am I. It works wonders."

"There's more to it." I explained that Peter was in a bit of a financial bind, how his plan was to fix up some of the properties and sell them at a profit. I told her that the idea was for me to do the landscaping and him to do the remodeling. "We'd be in business together."

"Hmm. Like Beyoncé and Jay Z."

I laughed. "Besides, it's only temporary. We'd rent out the house in Fairfax with the intention of coming back."

She studied my face. "So if it's such a great plan, why don't you look happier?"

Good question. "I guess I don't feel like Peter and I are very much of a team these days. The fact that I had to find out about his financial troubles from the police—I just can't forgive him for that."

Sonia nodded.

"And . . . I don't know . . . I just feel restless."

"This wouldn't have anything to do with a certain handsome Frenchman, would it?"

I could feel my face getting hot. "It's not that. It's . . . Things just haven't been the same with Peter and me since Thalia died. He's very sweet. He says all the right things. But I just feel . . . a distance between us."

"Oh, that doesn't mean a thing," Sonia responded. "It's impossible to feel passionate about a man all the time. I mean, it might be feasible if they just tried, but they don't understand the need for romance. They leave their dirty underwear on the floor and they fart and they watch stupid TV shows. It's like they *want* you to stop being attracted to them."

"Peter doesn't do that."

"Peter doesn't fart?"

"Not in front of me."

"Consider yourself extraordinarily lucky," Sonia said.

CHAPTER 19

As I folded laundry later that evening, I ruminated. If Marcel had left Dr. Lee's shop by five, what had he been doing between then and the time he arrived in a taxi at the hotel at 8:45? I wondered how I could find out where the taxi had picked him up. Something nagged at me, and then I remembered. I'd snatched two Yellow Cab receipts from Marcel's hotel room. With luck, one of them would be for the ride on September 1. I hurried upstairs and extracted them from a pile of papers on my desk. Yep. A receipt from September 1, printed at 8:21 p.m.—complete with vehicle number!

Armed with that information, I phoned Yellow Cab, claiming to have left my phone in the back seat on September 1. I described the time of the ride and gave him the car's number.

"You remember the number?" the dispatcher asked with surprise.

"I have a receipt," I explained. "My accountant tells me, always get a receipt."

"Hmm. Let me see. Cab eight-eight-nine, that's Dominic Yovino. No, Dom didn't turn in anything that day. It's possible you lost it somewhere else."

"Are you sure?" I asked, after a pause. "Maybe he didn't see it."

"We clean the cabs every twenty-four hours, lady. If there was a phone back there, we'd find it."

"OK, well, thanks for your help."

At least I had a name. Maybe I could track down this Dominic Yovino and ask him if he remembered where he'd picked up Marcel. Short of breaking into Yellow Cab's office and checking their records, I couldn't think of any other solution.

Maybe Sonia knew someone at Yellow Cab. She seemed to know people everywhere. I called her and explained my problem. "Nope, sorry, I have no inside connections in the taxi world," she said. "Oh, wait, I have an idea. Why don't we book a cab and ask for this Dominic guy to drive us?"

"Huh?"

"I'll do it," she said with excitement. "I'll say he's our favorite and we want Dominic. The shop's closed on Wednesday, right? We'll do it then. Pack a carry-on bag. We'll have him take us to the airport."

"The airport?" I protested, thinking of the cost of this excursion.

"It has to be done," she said firmly. "Yellow Cab won't come to Marin, so we'll need to get picked up in the city. And we can't just go a few blocks. I need time to get the information out of him, right? With any luck, we'll get stuck in traffic and have plenty of time to talk."

Frankly I was relieved that she was the one handling this. If anyone could get a man to open up, it was Sonia. The next few days passed quickly, with the shop demanding all of my attention. When Wednesday rolled around, Sonia picked me up bright and early. We drove to Liberty Street in the Castro neighborhood and pulled into the driveway of a Victorian cottage.

"Why here?" I asked.

"It's a friend's house. He's at work already, so I can park in his driveway. Come on." We waited out front, clutching our fake carry-ons. Sonia had even draped a foam travel pillow around her neck to look flight-ready. At ten minutes after nine, Yellow Cab number 889 pulled up.

"Good morning, ladies," said the driver, getting out to grab our bags. He was a small, wiry man with a mischievous smile. We climbed into the back seat. The radio was turned up loud, blaring a sports show. "SFO, right? Domestic terminal?"

"Yep."

"I figured, since you have no suitcases. Where you headed?"

"Phoenix," Sonia answered without missing a beat. She was good at this. She waited until he'd zipped up San Jose Avenue and was merging onto the 280 freeway before she launched into her story. "We asked for you specifically, you know. A friend of ours hailed your cab the other night, and he said you were great. A fast driver."

"That's me. Speedy." As if to prove it, he changed lanes with a burst of acceleration, causing the car he'd cut off to honk loudly. I clutched the door handle.

"I bet you remember him," Sonia continued. "He was from France."

"I don't know. We get a lot of tourists in the city."

"He went to the Jameson Hotel on Sacramento Street," Sonia prompted.

"Oh, yeah. Yeah, I remember that guy." Dominic was so close to the car in front of us that I was sure we were going to plow into it. But getting the hint, the driver moved over a lane, allowing our cab to roar ahead. "He was in a hurry to get to a meeting with his boss," Dominic continued. "Funny time of day for a meeting." He was doing about eighty-five now, passing cars with abandon.

"You picked him up near Golden Gate Park, right?" Sonia asked.

"Nah. Nah, I don't think so. Wait, let me think." I didn't want him thinking about anything other than his driving, but what could I do? "No, no, I picked him up on Geary. Yeah, I remember. Geary and Arguello. It was raining pretty hard."

I quickly calculated. That would be about a ten-minute drive. And if he'd started walking right after he killed Thalia, the timing would fit. Maybe he was going to walk back to the hotel, but it was taking too long, so he hailed a cab.

We passed Candlestick Park, prompting a spirited discussion between Dominic and Sonia about the 49ers. She managed to sound like a diehard fan, despite having no interest in football that I was aware of. We made it to the airport in record time. "What airline, ladies?"

"United," I said at exactly the same time Sonia said, "American."

"Oh, that's right, American," I giggled, hoping to convince him that I was just scatterbrained, rather than lying. Dominic pulled up in front of the terminal and hopped out to get our bags. I paid the fare plus a nice tip. Sonia batted her eyelashes at him and thanked him profusely. I thought she was going to hug him. As he roared away, I told Sonia that I was not going to shell out another fifty-plus bucks for the ride back. We took the BART train and then a city bus back to Sonia's car.

CHAPTER 20

I was sitting in the living room working on an order of French wine glasses for the shop when the phone rang. It was Sonia: "Good. You're home. Go turn on Channel Four."

"Why?" I asked.

"Just do it. Quick!"

The evening news was on. Captain Ryken was once again on the steps of Park Station, facing the camera. He said, "It would be premature to announce an arrest in the murder of Thalia Holcombe. All I can say is that we have a suspect in custody for possession of stolen property. We haven't made any further charges yet." He smiled telegenically. "We expect to have more news for you in the next several days." With that, he turned and walked into the building.

My thoughts were racing. Had they extradited Marcel from France? The camera cut to a reporter on the scene. "As you heard," the woman said, "the police aren't yet ready to link the man in custody to Thalia Holcombe's murder. All we know at this point is that Fred Gibson has a prior arrest record and that he was found in possession of items that belonged to the victim. Back to you, John."

What? Who the hell was Fred Gibson? By now the news had

switched to a robbery in Clayton, and I sat on the couch dumfounded. This made no sense. Was Fred Gibson an accomplice? I immediately dialed Hernandez's number, stuttered out an incoherent message, and hung up without saying goodbye.

I tried Garrett's number at home. No answer. I dialed his cell and got voice mail. Peter came downstairs to find me cursing. He asked what was wrong.

"Dammit. The police arrested someone for Thalia's murder."

He looked astonished, then pleased. "That's great news! Really great news. But why are you so angry?"

"Because," I said, "they've arrested someone named Fred Gibson!"

Peter looked confused. "So? What's wrong with that?"

"Don't be ridiculous. He didn't even know Thalia!" I was furious at how dense my husband was being. "They have the wrong person," I said fiercely.

Peter rolled his eyes. "Look, why don't you just let the police do their job? I'm sure they know what they're doing. It's not up to you to solve the crime."

"Apparently it is, since the police seem incapable." I hurried upstairs to the bedroom, shaking with anger. "Thalia, I'm sorry," I whispered. "I'm sorry this is all going so wrong. But I'll fix it, I promise." The phone rang again downstairs, and I heard Peter answer it. In a few minutes he came up to the bedroom.

"That was Garrett. The police told him the news. Fred Gibson was found trying to pawn Thalia's diamond bracelet. He claimed to have stumbled on the body after she was already dead. He's a homeless guy—lives in the park."

My fury at the police waned. It made perfect sense that they had arrested this Gibson guy. How could they do anything else, since he had Thalia's bracelet in hand? But that didn't mean he had killed her, I reminded myself. Maybe, as he claimed, he had just found her dead and helped himself to her jewelry.

Peter went on. "Garrett doesn't want to get too excited, but I can tell he's feeling hopeful that they've got the right guy."

"That's good," I said docilely. I didn't want to fight about it anymore. "I hope this is the end of the ordeal for Garrett."

"Me too. Want some dinner?" Peter asked. "I'm going to grill some burgers."

"Maybe later. I need to finish this glassware order." I tried to work, but I couldn't let go of this latest development. Could I have been wrong? What if this homeless man really did kill Thalia? Maybe it *was* a robbery. This randomness of the murder was profoundly disturbing to me, for reasons I couldn't fathom. No, I reassured myself. It was someone from France who was responsible. It had to be, because of the blackmail notes.

I turned on my laptop and began looking for information about extradition agreements between France and the United States, but everything I read was couched in legalese. Giving up, I went downstairs for dinner, still unsure about whether the real murderer could even be brought to justice, assuming I found some kind of proof.

Steering clear of Fred Gibson as a topic of discussion, Peter and I actually had a pleasant evening. At about ten, I climbed into bed with my laptop. I was reading about criminals who had been caught and convicted after years, sometimes decades, when I heard Peter coming up the stairs. I quickly turned off the light, set the laptop on the floor, and slid from seated to flat under the covers, eyes closed. I was in no mood for sex, and the headache excuse was too clichéd to even consider.

I lay as still as I could, as I heard him come into the room and undress. I knew he was folding his clothes and laying them over the back of the chair, as he did every night. He went into the bathroom. The water ran. I adjusted my position, facing away from his side of the bed. After a few minutes, the bathroom light snapped off and he slid under the covers beside me.

I hadn't been much in the sex department since the murder, but I couldn't bring myself to fake enthusiasm I didn't feel. Was I a terrible wife?

Peter stroked my arm. "Baby, wake up," he said softly.

I didn't move a muscle and even began lightly snoring, which I thought was a nice touch.

"Wake up," Peter said again. He was pressing against me now and kissing my neck. I turned toward him and put my arms around him. Despite myself, I was becoming aroused as Peter stroked my breasts and slipped inside me. It had been more than a week since we'd made love.

When it was over, I nestled in his arms, happy that things were back to normal. I was nearly asleep when a thought jolted me awake. I knew why Garrett had withdrawn all that money. "Peter. Peter, wake up."

"What's going on?" he asked sleepily.

"That money that the police asked Garrett about. It was for you, wasn't it?"

"Mmm."

"Peter," I scolded. "Why didn't you tell the police? How could you let Garrett come under suspicion?"

"What are you talking about?" He was wide-awake now. "The police never asked. And I never told Garrett not to tell them! All I asked was that he not tell *you*. I didn't want you to worry."

"Oh," I said in a small voice. "I'm sorry."

"Damn it, Rae, you're acting like a crazy person. First you

refuse to have sex. You think the police are idiots. And now you wake me up so you can yell at me. What the hell is going on with you?"

"I'm sorry."

He got up and grabbed his pillow. "I'm going downstairs to sleep on the couch."

CHAPTER 21

I took an early morning yoga class before work, hoping to clear my mind of Fred Gibson and my fight with Peter. For the most part, it worked, and I stepped out of the studio feeling virtuous. Jasper, tied up out front, was wagging his tail in response to the attentions of a passerby. After exchanging a few pleasantries with her, I popped into the coffeehouse on the corner for a latte and a muffin to go. Then I drove to Le Jardin with the dog, not bothering to change clothes, since the shop wasn't open that day.

The latte fueled me through several hours of paperwork. When all the bills were paid and filed, I turned my attention to the shelves, rearranging as I dusted. Things were looking a little bare. Ruefully, I realized Thalia had spent too much time with lover boy on her so-called buying trip and not enough time scouting merchandise. She'd left me in a bind. I'd need to get to some estate sales soon, since I couldn't go abroad right now.

Or could I? I was the boss, after all. True, the police had cautioned me to stick around. But it wasn't as if I were on a no-fly list or anything. How would they know if I left? No, I told myself sternly, I'd just come back to work. And the business really shouldn't be spending all that money on another trip to France. OK, that settled it. I was staying put.

Ready for a break, I walked with Jasper to the nursery down the street and bought some fragrant herbs to spruce up the containers on the patio. On the way back, I stopped at my favorite deli, but instead of my usual takeout salad, I opted for a huge cream-filled donut, telling myself that my morning yoga exertions cancelled out the calories.

As soon as we got back to the shop, I devoured the donut. Coffee. I needed coffee. I brewed a pot and then set to work planting the herbs. The dog sprawled in the sun while I worked. I envied his serenity. Not a care in the world. He barely blinked when I turned on the hose.

Now with caffeine and sugar sending me into overdrive, I decided to update the window display. It was time to replace the summery vignette of a table set for an al fresco lunch. I briefly considered delaying until tomorrow when Susan would be at work to help, but I was too antsy to wait. Removing the party lights strung overhead, the dishes, and the table and chairs didn't take long. I laid down a wool kilim rug that I'd bought at an estate sale, then dragged a vintage French leather chair to the window. Maneuvering the bulky chair took a while, and my back protested. But at last it was where I wanted it. I added a floor lamp, a small bookcase (I'd bring some books from home to fill it), and an iron fireplace screen embellished with curlicues. Jasper promptly lay down on the rug. I stepped outside to survey my handiwork.

Perfect, especially with the dog completing the cozy tableau. I had to admit, much as I missed Thalia, it felt good to be running the business myself. I'd need to add another salesperson now that she was gone. But I'd already lined up two people to interview tomorrow for a bookkeeping job.

I was back at the computer placing table linen orders when

Peter called, apologetic about last night's argument. "I'm sorry I snapped at you," he said. "You were right. I phoned Garrett today and insisted that he tell the police the money was for me."

"You did? That's terrific."

"No more secrets. I promise." Peter offered to make amends by taking me out to dinner at my favorite Italian restaurant. Naturally, I said yes. I suspected a discussion of Arizona would be on the agenda, but the prospect of house-made gnocchi and a big glass of vino won out.

First, though, I had a few errands to run. At the dry cleaners, the young woman ahead of me in line carried a sleeping baby in a front pack. All that was visible was a mop of dark hair and chubby legs clad in stripes. I smiled at the mother and we talked for a minute.

As I got back in the car with my plastic-wrapped dry cleaning, I thought again about Thalia's pregnancy. Surely she hadn't known. Wouldn't she have told me? I had to admit that if she wasn't planning to have the baby—as Hernandez had speculated—that might not have been something she'd want to share. The question of whether or not Thalia knew nagged at me. I still had a few hours before I needed to meet Peter. I dropped the dog off at home and drove into the city.

The chic, gray-haired receptionist at the ob-gyn on California Street expressed her condolences when I told her I was a friend of Thalia's. "Thank you," I said. "The reason I stopped by is that I was in the neighborhood and was wondering if the doctor is accepting new patients. Thalia always spoke so highly of her that I've considered switching gynecologists."

"I'll check with her, but I think we're at capacity," the receptionist said with regret. "Of course, we're always happy to give you a referral."

Actually, I had no intention of switching doctors, but I feigned disappointment. "Oh, dear. Thalia was so fond of Dr. Alvarez. In fact, I think she had been in for an appointment shortly before her death." I paused and tried to sound mournful. "You know, to confirm the news."

"Yes, of course. That's what makes it even more tragic," said the receptionist, shaking her head. "Two lives lost." Aha. So Thalia *did* know. My first reaction was anger that she hadn't confided in me, but I squelched it. There was time to stew over that revelation later.

"I suppose she was overjoyed at the news," I said. "I mean, I know she'd been trying for some time."

"Oh, yes, she immediately made a phone call and sounded so excited." The woman sighed. "What a horrible turn of events. I hope they catch whoever did it and charge him with two murders."

I murmured my agreement, then asked casually, "Do you happen to know who Thalia called to share her good news?"

"No, I'm sorry, I don't. You know, the police asked me the very same thing. I assume it was her husband. Is he Italian? I think she was speaking Italian." She smiled. "Now, if you'd like a referral to a doctor, there's someone else in the building I can recommend." She handed me a business card, which I pocketed.

So Thalia had known she was pregnant and had shared the news with someone. Someone who spoke French, I was sure— Thalia didn't speak Italian. I considered the possibilities. Etienne? Luc? Her mother? I needed to tell Hernandez about this. But I wasn't ready to call him and have my theories dismissed yet again.

"She was a wonderful lady," the woman continued. "What a tragedy. She was so overcome with emotion at the news, especially after she spoke to her husband. She was weeping. So many women break down, you know, after trying for so long."

I thanked her and said goodbye, crumpling up the referral she'd given me as soon as I got to the car. What if Thalia's tears had not been of the joyful variety? I wondered. Suppose she had called Etienne, and he had not been pleased at their looming parenthood? That could sour their relationship, couldn't it? But that certainly wasn't a reason for him to kill her!

I mentally reviewed everyone's whereabouts on the night of the murder. Etienne had been in Sausalito talking to a rug merchant. Or so he said. And Renata had stayed at the hotel. Naturally, the police would have confirmed all that. But it wouldn't hurt to double-check.

CHAPTER 22

"Thalia was pregnant," I announced to Sonia.

"What! When did she tell you?"

"She didn't." I explained that I'd found out from Garrett, who'd been told by the police. "And this is the worst part—at least for Garrett. Etienne was the father."

"No! Did they do a DNA test?"

"Yes. But they didn't need to. Based on how far along she was, she got pregnant in France."

"Oh my God. This just keeps getting worse."

We sat in silence for a while, sipping coffee in Sonia's backyard. The resident goat was munching on Sonia's ailing rosebush, and Jasper was snoozing in the sun with Sonia's two dogs, worn out from romping.

"She told Etienne," I said. "At least I think she did. All I know is she called someone as soon as she found out." I filled Sonia in about my visit to the gynecologist. "The receptionist said she was happy at the news. But I know Thalia was still smoking and drinking, even after she found out. So she couldn't have been planning to continue the pregnancy." Sonia nodded. "I'm guessing Etienne said he didn't want any part of it," I said.

Sonia winced. "Harsh as it is, it kind of makes sense that he wouldn't want to have a child with Thalia," she said. "That would really be a messy situation."

"Yeah. You know, I don't think Etienne was as committed to her as Thalia thought. First of all, he brought his family along to her house. Why would he do that? And then you told me how he was flirting with you." I shook my head ruefully. "I don't know. Maybe to him it was just a fling."

"Maybe. Poor Thalia."

After a minute I said, "Do you think Etienne could have killed her?"

"What? No! Thalia was mugged in the park. Why would you think Etienne did that?"

"Well if Thalia was going to have his baby—"

"You just said she wasn't," Sonia pointed out.

"OK, OK," I conceded. "But what if he didn't know that? Or what if Renata found out and she made a stink, threatened to leave him? She's the one with the money, so he might be desperate to hang on to her. I need to check both of their alibis for the night of the murder."

"Don't you think the police have done that?"

"Sure. But they're not infallible."

"Sweetie, I think you're becoming a little obsessed. Thalia was in the park after dark, and she was mugged by Fred Gibson. Can't you just accept that?"

"No. Not yet. How about you ask your new pal Detective Levine about Renata and Etienne's alibis?"

She shook her head. "You know he can't discuss the case with me."

"OK, then ask him more generally. Ask him how they check

alibis. Then steer it around to the Duchamps somehow. Use your charms."

Sonia rolled her eyes. "I'll see what I can find out."

Peering through the plate-glass window, I spied a small, olive-skinned man seated at a gleaming mahogany desk. I knocked on the door. He rose to his feet and hurried to let me in.

"How do you do," said Mr. Akbari.

"Thank you for meeting with me after hours. It's difficult for me to get away from my shop."

"Of course. Would you care for some tea?"

I accepted, and he poured me a glass of fragrant mint tea from a small pot that rested on a brass tray. The store was more like an art gallery than a rug shop. A selection of plush carpets covered the center of the gleaming wood floor. The walls had thick wooden shelves holding dozens of rolled-up rugs.

Mr. Akbari motioned to two leather chairs with a small table in between. I sat. Clearly, this was a shop where customers took their time and personal attention was paramount.

"I very much enjoyed meeting your friend Etienne," said Mr. Akbari. "I appreciate his referring you."

"Yes, he's a lovely man," I agreed.

We chatted for a few minutes, then got down to business—the business I had concocted as an excuse to meet. I explained that every once in a while, when I made purchases for the shop at estate sales, I came upon a beautiful rug. But since that wasn't my area of expertise, I didn't know how to price the rugs for sale in the shop. At Etienne's recommendation, I was hoping Mr.

Akbari could help me. "Would you be willing to do the occasional valuation if I brought a rug to you?"

"Of course, of course, my dear. It would be my pleasure."

When I confessed that my knowledge of Oriental rugs was somewhat spotty, Mr. Akbari launched into an in-depth tutorial, pulling out merchandise in various styles as examples. I spent nearly an hour learning about knotting techniques, dyes, and the origins of different motifs. It was fascinating stuff. "Come, I have a treasure I must show you." He led me into the back room. "This one has been purchased by a decorator for a high-end client. She's picking it up tomorrow." He unfurled a breathtaking carpet with every shade of blue mingling with deep red and chestnut. "Feel it," he urged. It was velvety soft. "This is from the Caucasus. Woven in the nineteenth century. It's in pristine condition. Rugs like this don't come my way often."

"Etienne must have enjoyed seeing your beautiful merchandise," I ventured.

"Yes, and he's quite knowledgeable. He told me that he has an eighteenth-century silk Kayseri in his bedroom in Paris."

"I wonder, did he have a chance to explore Sausalito when he was here?"

"We went for an early dinner, and I showed him the downtown. But he left soon after. He was eager to get back to his family. He's very devoted to his wife, you know. He told me all about the trip to Bali he was going to surprise her with for their twenty-fifth anniversary." Oh, dear. I wondered what Thalia would have thought of that. Mr. Akbari continued, "I do hope he didn't get stuck in traffic. It was about seven, so that shouldn't have been too bad."

"No, not too bad," I agreed, calculating that Etienne could have easily made it to the murder site in Golden Gate Park by eight if traffic was light. But wait, Julien said he'd returned to the hotel at 7:45. Could he have left again? Presumably, the police had confirmed all this.

Feeling like I'd wasted my time, and too tired to even think about checking Renata's alibi, I hoped that maybe Sonia would have some luck getting intel from Detective Levine.

When I got home, I got out my laptop to finish up a few work-related things, then checked my personal email. There was a message from Julien asking me to call him right away. A string of exclamation points reinforced the urgency. I checked the time. It was very early morning in Paris. He might still be asleep, but the exclamation points won out. Julien answered on the third ring.

"I saw Marie Resnais," he said excitedly as soon as he heard my voice.

"Who?"

"She's the person Marcel replaced at my father's company." He went on to tell me how Marie had given notice abruptly, claiming she needed to move to Dijon to take care of her ailing grandmother. She'd referred Marcel as a replacement, saying he was an old family friend. "But I saw her riding her bicycle here in Paris," Julien said. "I'm sure it was her."

"Maybe she was just in town for the day," I said, frankly disappointed that this was the big news. "Or maybe her grandmother died and she moved back."

"Maybe. But I don't think so. I was on the bus, and I called out to her as she passed. She turned toward me, then as soon as she recognized me, she put her head down and sped off. Something isn't right. I'm going to try to find out where she lives and talk to her."

I wasn't convinced of the significance of his encounter, but Julien was clearly excited. "OK, but be careful," I cautioned. "If this person is mixed up with Marcel, it could be dangerous."

CHAPTER 23

A few days after the Marie Resnais sighting, I heard from Julien again. "Guess what?" he said excitedly. "Jerome is going to visit the Legrande warehouse next month." I remembered that name from the papers I'd spied in Marcel's hotel room. "He's negotiating a new lease. And Marcel talked his way into the trip. He said he has a relative in Nice, and he's going to combine the warehouse visit with a vacation in the south. Jerome seemed very annoyed, but my father agreed to it. So then I told my father I want to go too."

"You?"

"Yes, why not?" He sounded offended. "I said I want to learn all about the business, since I'll be taking it over some day. Of course, that's not true," he said with a laugh. "But I just know that something big is happening in Marseille, and I want to find out what it is."

So did I. Fred Gibson was still in custody, the police had made no further announcements, Sonia had been unable to pry any information out of Levine, and I was feeling that Thalia's murder might never be solved. The business couldn't really afford it, but I was taking a trip to France. I didn't know what I expected to accomplish with the journey, but I felt compelled to go.

Three weeks later, I was blearily riding up the snaking escalators at Charles de Gaulle Airport. I had barely slept on the eleven-hour flight. Now my all-nighter was catching up with me as I made my way to the Métro for the twenty-five-minute journey into the city.

Leaving town wasn't as hard as I'd feared. Sonia was helping out Susan at the shop, and I'd hired a new person, as well. I wasn't sure if the police still expected me to stick around, but since they had a suspect in custody, I decided they wouldn't miss me. Better to ask for forgiveness than permission, right?

The other hurdle I'd anticipated was Peter, but, to my surprise, he didn't object. Of course, I didn't tell him about pursuing Marcel. As far as he knew, my trip was purely business. Oh, and I also left out another little detail: I'd called Luc and arranged for him to accompany me and Julien to Marseille. Since it was his sister whose murder we were trying to solve, it was only natural that he should be included. At least that's what I told myself, realizing that Peter was unlikely to see it that way.

So there I was on the other side of the Atlantic. I emerged from the Métro at Gare du Nord into the chilly air of an October morning, hailed a cab, and settled in as the driver took me to the Fifth Arrondissement. The streets looked dirtier and more crowded since my last visit two years ago. But Paris was still Paris. A short nap, I thought, and then I'd have the whole day to wander at leisure. I'd start my sleuthing in earnest tomorrow. I still had more than a week ahead of me before the trip to Marseille.

The hotel was exactly as I remembered it from prior visits. After checking in, I squeezed into the tiny elevator with my suitcase and ascended to my room on the second floor. I liked this room because it faced the street and had a balcony. In any other city, I might have preferred a quieter locale, but I found the bustling street below intoxicating. I flung open the tall casement windows and drank in the scene, the flower stands, the bakery that made the most incredible brioches, the corner pharmacy stocked with glamorous beauty potions. Sighing with pleasure, I decided to forgo the nap.

I considered phoning Peter but realized he'd be asleep. Later, I decided. Then I spent a few leisurely hours roaming the neighborhood, stopping at the Tuesday market on rue Mouffetard to buy some fruit and cheese. I carried my provisions to the Luxembourg Gardens, where I found a vacant bench. Before eating, I phoned Luc. "I've arrived," I announced.

"Welcome. I'm coming to Paris on Thursday."

"You are?" I said, delighted by the thought of spending time with Luc ahead of the Marseille journey. Purely to plan our strategy, of course.

"Yes. I'm going to stay in town for a few days to attend to business. And then perhaps I can spirit you away to the farm before we head down south."

"I'd love that," I said. We arranged to meet for dinner on Thursday. I unwrapped my parcel of Brie and grapes and slowly savored my meal as I watched two young boys throw crumbs to a cluster of sparrows. After lunch, I phoned Julien, who invited me to meet him at his father's office on Thursday at noon. I wrote down the directions. "I found Marie Resnais on Facebook, and I think I've finally figured out where she works," he said proudly. "I'm going to try to find her. I want to talk to her in person. Oh, and I told my father you were in town. He's insisting that you come to dinner at our house. My mother will call you tomorrow."

I walked for another two hours, soaking up the sights and musing about the wisdom of sitting down to dinner with Thalia's former lover and his wife. Things could get awkward. Maybe

Julien could wangle an invitation for Luc, too. That might take some of the pressure off. Finally, at four o'clock, my feet aching, I went back to the hotel, intending to nap for an hour. When I opened my eyes again, I was astonished to see that it was nine o'clock the following morning.

I had never called Peter! I sent him an email telling him all was well. I had a voice mail from Hernandez, asking me to call him back, but I ignored it. Then I showered, dressed, and went downstairs to the breakfast room off the hotel lobby. A smiling waitress with a North African accent poured me a steaming cup of coffee and brought a small pitcher of warm milk. Across the room, an array of pastries, yogurt, and juices was set out. I chatted with a German couple at the next table about the hills of San Francisco, taking my time over a flaky croissant and a second cup of coffee. Then I walked up the winding marble staircase rather than taking the elevator. If I was going to be eating croissants every morning, I'd better get some exercise.

I gathered some things and set off across town to the small and very posh Hôtel Sainte Bernadette. I approached the gleaming mahogany front desk, illuminated by a crystal chandelier. "Hello. I'm wondering if you can help me," I said in French to the man on duty. "I'm a friend of one of your regular guests, Thalia Holcombe."

"Ah, Madame Holcombe," said the man, nodding. "Yes, yes, of course. How is she?" he asked with a smile.

"I'm afraid I have some sad news," I said. "She met with an accident. She died last month."

"*Mon Dieu!*" the man exclaimed. "I'm terribly sorry to hear that. She was very well liked by the staff. My condolences."

"Thank you. I'm trying to track down a friend of hers, someone who may have come to see her here at the hotel." I took out a picture of Marcel, which I'd printed at home. "Do you remember this man coming to see her the last time she was here? I have something of Thalia's that I need to give to him."

He looked at the photo carefully and shook his head. "No, I don't recall seeing this gentleman. But perhaps someone else who works here has seen him. Would you like to leave the photo?"

I hesitated. I should have made photocopies. "All right," I said. "But I'll need it back. It's the only one I have."

"Certainly, madame. Come back for it whenever you like." He wrote down my cell phone number. "I'll be sure to ask the rest of the staff if they know of this gentleman."

As I left, I wondered if they had video surveillance cameras aimed at the front desk like American hotels and, if so, whether there was any way to get a look at the tape from a month ago. Did they even keep those tapes? Once again, I was struck by just how little I knew about detective work.

Feeling discouraged, I decided it was time for fortification. I stopped at the first café I passed and ordered an espresso. Somehow I'd thought the visit would be more productive, that someone would have recognized Marcel and remembered that he'd brought a note for Thalia. It had been nearly two months ago, I reminded myself. Maybe whoever worked that night didn't even work at the Sainte Bernadette anymore. Well, at least they had Marcel's photo. Maybe someone would remember him.

My thoughts turned to what to wear when I met Luc for dinner, followed by a twinge of guilt for focusing on fashion when I was supposed to be investigating Thalia's murder and shopping for Le Jardin. OK, time to scout out some merchandise. I took the Métro to Village Saint-Paul in the Marais district, where numerous antique dealers were clustered in the network of quaint courtyards and alleyways.

It was a productive excursion. My big finds were two oversize mirrors with gilded frames and a fabulous iron child's bed. I also snapped up as much enamelware as I could find, since my customers loved it: coffee pots, pitchers, kitchen utensil sets.

Anything with French writing on it was always a hit too, no matter how beat-up. I found several old gas station signs in beautiful condition that I knew would fetch a good price. I finished the day shopping for garden decor: a marble-topped bistro table, some terra-cotta urns with a weathered patina, a dozen olive baskets, and a pair of decorative iron gates. Le Jardin's credit card got a good workout. I arranged to have everything shipped back.

Pleased with my finds, I decided to indulge in a little shopping for myself. When I finally boarded the train back to my hotel, I had a shockingly expensive but absolutely gorgeous new pair of leather boots with me.

CHAPTER 24

I checked my watch as I hurried along rue Norvins on Thursday. I was due to meet Julien in five minutes. As I approached Etienne's office building, a man who looked like Marcel stepped out onto the street. I ducked into the nearest doorway. As he passed, I got a closer look. It was most definitely Marcel, wearing dark slacks and a tan zip-up jacket. On an impulse, I decided to follow him.

I stayed close behind as he retraced the route I had just walked and descended into the Abbesses Métro station. It took me a minute to fumble for my ticket, but when I got to the platform, he was still there. A train was just pulling in.

I watched him board, then got in two cars behind him. Now what? How would I know when he got off? I stood near the doors, even though there were plenty of seats available. As the train picked up speed, I phoned Julien. "Sorry, I'm going to be late. I'm following Marcel."

"I can barely hear you," he said. "What's all that noise?"

"I'm on the Métro. I'm following Marcel," I said louder. "I'll come later. Can you go to lunch later?"

"Yes. Sure."

"Good. Ciao." I hung up. When the train stopped at the next

station, I poked my head out the door, scanning all the passengers disembarking. Not seeing my quarry, I released the door and pulled my head back in. The train started up again. I repeated the move at the next stop and again at the third. There he was! I slipped through the doors and followed him, keeping my eyes on his tan jacket. He rode the escalator to the platform for the Line Four train heading north. I kept my distance. Once I was certain he was going to stay put, I turned my back to him as we waited for the train. When it pulled in, I again got on two cars behind him. This train was nearly empty, with only two stops to go until the end of the line. Marcel got off at the last stop, Porte de Clignancourt. I followed him up the stairs.

I knew this area of Paris well. Les Puces—the flea market at Clignancourt—was one of my spots to scout out merchandise for the shop. Bargains were scarce, but the quality was good at many of the vendors. I followed Marcel through the crowd of stalls on the perimeter of the market. Here, vendors hawked T-shirts, knockoffs of pricey running shoes, watches, and all manner of junk. After a few blocks, we reached rue des Rosiers and entered the flea market proper, which was actually a hodgepodge of fourteen different markets, each crammed with shops and stalls. Some markets specialized in art, some in furniture, others in books. I had my favorite vendors, some of whom knew me by name. But this was no time for browsing. I kept my eye on Marcel's tan jacket, staying about twenty feet behind him. He made several turns through the narrow alleys, walking rapidly. I cursed my new French boots, which were starting to pinch.

Finally, he entered a small shop. Painted on the none-too-clean front window was *Arts de l'Orient* in gold and black lettering. Behind the glass was a jumble of Asian artifacts: gold-leafed painted screens, porcelain figurines, a large brass gong. I peered in. Among the clutter, I could see Marcel. He was standing in front of a glass case on the far wall, talking to a silver-haired woman and pointing at something in the case. She opened the case and handed him an object, which he examined, then handed back. After the woman locked the case, Marcel pulled a manila envelope out of his jacket and handed it to her. They turned toward the front of the shop, and I pulled my head back so I was concealed from view behind the gong. When I dared to look again, the two were standing by the front counter. Marcel's back was to the door, and the woman was behind the counter, facing the street. She tucked the envelope below the counter, near the cash register. Words were exchanged, then Marcel turned toward the front door. I scampered away, ducking into the next shop.

I waited a moment before peeking out. No sign of Marcel. I entered Arts de l'Orient, whose aisles were as crammed with merchandise as the front window. The woman behind the counter smiled. "May I help you, madame?" she asked in French.

"I think I just saw a friend of mine leaving," I said. "Was a man named Marcel just in here?"

The woman pursed her lips. "I don't know the gentleman's name," she said. "He was here to see my boss."

At this I had no further ideas. "OK. Thanks." I browsed, trying to get an inkling of what Marcel had been after. I strolled over to the display case that he had seemed interested in. It was filled with figurines carved of jade, ivory, and wood.

"May I show you something?" the woman asked.

"These are lovely," I said, desperate for inspiration to strike.

"Your friend is quite the collector," the woman volunteered.

"Yes. Yes he is," I said, hoping I didn't sound moronic. Then I added, with a coy smile. "Actually, he's more than a friend." The woman smiled in return. "*Ah, oui.*"

"I'd love to surprise him with something. For his birthday. Was there anything in particular he admired?"

The woman unlocked the case and removed a small carving of a Chinese island village, exquisitely detailed, right down to the miniature men poling rafts through the water.

"How much is that?"

"Seven hundred euros."

I was shocked but tried not to show it.

"It's ivory, of course," said the woman.

"Of course." I stared at the carving, feeling it was important to buy it if I was going to gain any more information from this woman. But how could I justify spending so much money?

"It's an antique," the woman said. "It dates back to the late 1800s."

Peter would kill me if he found out what it cost. I could always sell it in the shop, I rationalized. That's what I'd do. I'd charge it on the business credit card and sell it. Peter wouldn't even know about it. "Very well, I'll take it," I said.

As the woman rang up the sale, she said, "Your friend will be disappointed when he comes back to find it's been sold."

"Oh, is he coming back?" I asked, trying to sound casual.

"I believe so. He wants my boss to phone him about some other ivory pieces."

"Well, please don't tell him I bought it. I want to surprise him."

"Don't worry, *chérie*, I won't say anything. Would you like me to wrap this for you?"

"No, thank you."

"It's no trouble. I have some ribbon in the back."

"All right, if you don't mind." The minute the woman disappeared through a curtained doorway, I scooted behind the counter. There was the envelope from Marcel. I grabbed it and stuffed it in my purse, feeling immensely guilty. I vowed that if there was money in it, I would mail it back.

The woman returned with the ribbon and proceeded to painstakingly wrap the carving in a small box. I was fervently hoping she wouldn't glance down and notice the envelope was gone. Finally, package in hand, I walked slowly out the door. As soon as I turned the corner, I broke into a run.

"Never!" Julien said emphatically. "My father would never condone poaching. It's impossible."

We sat at an outdoor table at a café near Etienne's office. Between us lay the letter that I'd snatched from Arts de l'Orient. We'd each read it twice. Julien had to help with some of the French, because it was written in convoluted language that avoided any outright mention of wrongdoing. Still, its meaning was clear: Marcel was offering a shipment of contraband ivory for sale. Apparently, he'd have the merchandise in hand sometime in the next ten days.

"It's got to be in the shipment coming in next week!" Julien said with excitement. "That's why Marcel has been so insistent on going to Marseille."

"And you're sure your parents are not involved in this?" Images of slaughtered elephants swam in my brain. An online search had revealed more than I'd ever wanted to know about the illegal ivory trade. Despite the ban on ivory, some ten thousand elephants are illegally killed each year for their tusks. The brutality was mind-boggling.

"Of course! That's why we can't call the police. They would shut down my father's business."

I suspected he was right. We sat silently as we considered

our next move. Finally, Julien said, "Let's stick with our original plan. We'll follow him to Marseille. Maybe he's picking up merchandise that has nothing to do with my father's company, which would be great. It's too soon to call the police."

"Maybe." I sincerely hoped Etienne wasn't involved in this. Thoughts of beheaded elephants came to mind again, but I pushed them aside. "OK. We'll go. But whether we discover anything or not, when we get back we need to tell the police. I can't let these poachers get away with this."

We discussed the logistics for the trip to Marseille. Luc and I would drive down on Wednesday and spend the night in a hotel near the waterfront. On Thursday, Julien would stick close to Marcel at the loading dock and warehouse until there was something to report, then he'd phone us.

I spent an hour getting dressed for dinner with Luc, changing my outfit repeatedly. When I had exhausted all the clothes in my suitcase, I went back to the first outfit, a black skirt and green cashmere sweater. Would perfume be too much? I didn't want to give the impression that I thought it was a date. My phone rang. It was Peter.

"So how's my little detective?" he asked.

"What? No, honey, I told you. I'm here for work. Sorry I didn't call you yesterday. I got to the hotel and slept all day."

"And how is the hotel? Do they still have those god-awful pillows?"

I laughed. Peter had stayed here with me on my last buying trip, and his only complaint was the single wide pillow per double bed. "Yes, of course. That's part of the charm. But the croissants are to die for. How's Jasper?"

"He's fine. I took him for a good run this morning. He hasn't moved since."

"And how's work?"

"Same old shit. I miss you."

"I miss you, too."

"Oh, I almost forgot. Hernandez called the house. He said you haven't returned his calls."

"Yeah, I don't want to be yelled at for leaving town." After a few more minutes we said goodbye, and I hurried off to meet Luc.

When I got to the restaurant, Luc was standing out front, dressed in khaki slacks and a pale orange linen shirt. I wondered if he was aware of how good he looked. We kissed on both cheeks, and he put his arm on my back as he held the door for me. This was most definitely feeling like a date.

After we ordered, I said, "I've been waiting all afternoon to tell you what I found out about Marcel. He—"

Luc held up a hand and smiled. "No talk of sleuthing until after dinner. It's not good for the digestion."

Oh God, the French and their food. With them, eating was akin to a sacrament. But I respected his request and changed the subject. The food was divine, as was the Bordeaux. Finally, when the plates were cleared and two snifters of cognac arrived, Luc clinked his glass against mine and said, "All right, now you may tell me about your adventures."

"I followed Marcel today," I began.

Luc's expression changed abruptly to a frown. "That sounds risky."

"I wasn't planning to. It just happened. I ran into him on the way to see Julien, and I decided to see where he went."

"And?"

"He went to Clignancourt. To a little shop that sells Asian antiques and bric-a-brac. He wanted to buy this." I paused for effect and took my time extracting the small box from my handbag, lifting the lid, and unwrapping the intricately carved figurine from its velvet cloth.

Luc emitted a low whistle. "How much did you pay for this?"

"Seven hundred euros."

"Why on earth . . . ?"

"It's evidence."

"Evidence of what?"

"It's real ivory."

"Yes, I surmised that from the price."

"Luc, he's smuggling ivory."

"Hold on. That's quite a leap from buying a figurine to trafficking in ivory."

"Read this," I said, pulling the envelope from my purse.

He spent a couple of moments reading. "How did you get this?" he asked.

"I snatched it. Are you proud of me?" I was feeling tipsy now.

"Very. So what are we to make of this?" Luc said.

As he continued reading through the material, I turned the carving around in my hand, studying it sadly. "Some poor elephant lost his life for this trinket."

"Do you think this ties in with my sister's murder?"

"It has to. You know she caught him snooping through Etienne's desk. He was only hired three months ago. What was he doing going through his boss's desk?"

"Hold on, hold on," Luc said. "Why would he try to extort money from Thalia if he was the one with the guilty secret? This isn't making sense."

Must he be so logical? I polished off my cognac. "Somehow, he was trying to get her out of Etienne's life. OK, maybe it wasn't the smartest move on his part. I'll give you that. But Marcel is clearly involved in something illegal. All I know is I'm committed to this trip to Marseille. I completely understand if you don't want to go along."

"If you're sure about the smuggling, call the police," Luc urged.

"No. Not yet. Julien and I don't want to create a scandal for Etienne if he isn't involved. Believe me, I know what that's like."

He sighed. "You're as stubborn as my sister, but in your own quiet way. Listen, I have a friend who works for the World Wildlife Fund. I'll call her tomorrow and see if she can find out anything."

"Wonderful! You can hang on to the letter."

He put it in his shirt pocket. "And now I have something to show you." He pulled a small silver picture frame out of his jacket pocket. Inside was a photo of Thalia and me, laughing on the beach.

"I took this when we went to Menton for the weekend. Remember?"

"Wow. We were so young!" Thalia wore an impossibly skimpy bikini. Her head was back and she was laughing. Her golden hair shone in the sun. I was convulsed with laughter too, looking less chic in my ill-fitting one-piece. Gazing at the photo, I felt a profound sense of loss.

He squeezed my hand. "That's for you to keep."

"Thank you."

He walked me back to my hotel. "Want to come up?" I asked. Inwardly I winced. What was I thinking!

"No, I'm pretty tired," he said, to my relief. "I'll call you in the morning."

CHAPTER 25

I exited the École Militaire station and headed north toward rue de Montessuy. It was only five blocks to the boxy apartment building where Etienne and Renata lived. The building looked anomalous between the grand eighteenth-century structures on either side of it. A concierge tipped his cap and directed me to the elevator. As I rode to the eighth floor, I was hoping Luc had already arrived. I wasn't sure what to expect at this little soiree, and I wanted his moral support.

Julien answered the door, wearing skinny jeans, a pinstripe shirt, and a tie. Before leading me into the living room, he whispered, "I want to tell you about Marie Resnais, but I can't talk about it now."

Four other guests sat in the living room, sipping drinks and nibbling hors d'oeuvres. In the far corner of the room, Etienne was pouring drinks. "Rae," he called out. "What can I get for you? A kir? Or would you prefer a glass of wine?"

At the same time, Renata came into the room and hurried over to kiss me on both cheeks. "Welcome to Paris," she said. "What can I get you to drink?"

"Wine, please. Red if you have it."

"Darling, get Rae a glass of Côtes du Rhône," Renata called

to Etienne. "Come, let me introduce you to everyone." She took me by the hand. "You know Marcel, of course, and Jerome. This is Jerome's friend Michelle"—the pretty young woman shook my hand—"and my very best friend, Angelique." As Renata continued, I smiled politely at each of them and exchanged pleasantries.

"What a marvelous view," I said as Etienne handed me a glass of wine. The wide swath of windows framed the upper half of the Eiffel Tower, with a hint of the green lawn of the Champ de Mars below it and the Seine curving behind it. In my opinion, a view like that would be best left unadorned. Instead, the windows had voluminous brocade valences and draperies, heavy with tassels. The rest of the room was furnished in a similar fashion, with overly large furniture, all matching. The couch and chair were upholstered in dark green velvet. Twin walnut end tables, each topped with an identical lamp, flanked the couch. Even the artwork consisted of matching pairs of prints in heavily carved gilded frames. Renata certainly liked symmetry.

I was talking with Angelique when the doorbell rang again. Julien hurried to answer it and came back into the room with Luc, who was holding a basket full of salad greens—from the farm, no doubt. "Julien, please take those lovely vegetables into the kitchen," Renata commanded. Introductions were once again made. Luc went over to the bar to chat with Etienne, and I resumed my conversation with Renata's friend.

"And how is it you know Renata and Etienne?" Angelique asked.

"Through business. My business partner did some work with Etienne."

"Oh, the woman who died."

"Yes," I said.

"I remember how annoyed Renata was that she had to skip several sights she wanted to see because of the investigation and the funeral. She complained about the police harassing her."

I said nothing, and Angelique looked contrite. "Oh, I'm sorry," she said. "I'm sure it was difficult for you, as well."

"Yes. Thank you." There was brief awkward silence, then Jerome joined us and talk turned to the current Magritte exhibit, which Jerome urged me to see. Angelique excused herself, and Jerome and I continued to chat about my plans during my visit. He recommended several new restaurants. I liked his quiet manner and noticed how comfortable I felt with him. I decided I better get down to business.

"So what's it like working with Marcel?" I asked.

He looked surprised. OK, so that wasn't the smoothest transition—but I didn't have all night. "Why do you ask?" Jerome said.

"Oh, well, he had only recently joined the company last time I saw you. I wondered how it was working out."

"He's very eager to learn," Jerome said. "He takes notes about everything. In fact, he insisted on accompanying me on my next trip to Marseille."

I helped myself to a radish and dipped it in a little dish of salt, trying to look nonchalant.

Jerome continued. "He says he wants to understand the import/export business because he's thinking of opening his own company in Corsica."

"Is that where he's from?"

Jerome nodded, and I asked about Corsica's reputation for drug smuggling.

"Oh, yes, that was in the 1980s," he said. "But that's all over now. Things have changed. It's quite lovely there."

Renata jingled a small glass bell and announced dinner. We

followed her to the dining room, where she directed us to our places. I was seated next to Luc. On my other side was Angelique. Marcel faced me across the table. This room had the same sort of oversized walnut furniture as the living room, and an even more spectacular view of the Eiffel Tower, which by this time blazed with illumination against the darkening sky.

Renata served soup, while Etienne poured wine. The meal proceeded at a leisurely pace, with no hurry to clear the plates between courses. When the salad was finally served (after the main course, in true French fashion), Renata gushed over the greens Luc had brought. There was heated conversation about the merits of organic produce. Talk turned to organic meat and the benefits of feeding beef cows grass rather than grain. Luc said, "Many people favor organic meat because it's raised more humanely." Jerome's girlfriend, who'd barely spoken until then, said, "I don't understand why people say we shouldn't eat meat. Our ancestors were hunters, after all." Another bottle was opened and my glass was refilled. I was feeling a bit woozy by now.

Emboldened by multiple glasses of very good wine, I seized the opportunity to lead the conversation to elephants—albeit somewhat awkwardly. "Well at least in this country there's no wholesale slaughter of animals in the wild. I was just reading that ninety-six elephants are illegally killed every day in Africa. Even though they're protected, there's so much bribery that poachers are able to operate freely."

"They don't eat them, do they?" asked Jerome's girlfriend.

"It's for ivory," I said. "They're beheaded, and their bodies are left to rot." I glanced at Julien, who looked aghast at where I was going with this. He hastily excused himself to see about dessert.

Jerome said quietly, "I know that in Kenya, some of the deaths are at the hands of farmers, not poachers. After all, people have to earn a livelihood, and they can't have elephants damaging their farmland."

Ignoring him, I addressed Marcel. "Marcel, what do you think? Should farmers be allowed to kill elephants?"

Marcel answered somewhat stiffly. "I've never thought about it. I'm not familiar with the situation in Kenya."

"Of course, the elephants were there first," I went on. "For many millions of years. Do you know that elephants cry when a member of their family is slain? Real tears."

"Very touching," Marcel said with what sounded like sarcasm, although I couldn't be sure. Luc put his foot on mine under the table. I knew I was going on too much, but I didn't want to stop. Besides, I liked the feel of Luc's foot and the way his calf pressed against mine.

I continued. "Do you know there was an elephant separated from a companion at a zoo. And twenty-five years later, they encountered each other again. And they remembered. They greeted each other with joy." Here my voice cracked a little, and I swallowed hard. The images I'd seen online earlier flooded my brain. I decided I'd better stop talking. Renata jumped into the silence with an anecdote about the family's trip to the Pyrenees last summer.

I excused myself and got up to find the bathroom. My passage down the hallway was a bit unsteady. Shutting the door behind me, I gripped the sink and stared at my reflection in the bathroom mirror. My face was flushed. I splashed cold water on my cheeks and attempted to smooth my hair. I wanted nothing more than for this evening to be over. As I emerged from the bathroom, I collided with Marcel, who was standing just outside the door. I gave a small scream.

"I'm sorry if I startled you," he said, but he made no move to let me pass.

"Pardon me," I said, trying to squeeze by him.

"Why are you here?" he said softly.

"Excuse me?" I wasn't sure I'd heard him correctly.

He repeated the question. "Why have you come to Paris?"

"I'm here on business," I answered, my heart thudding.

His face was close to mine, and his gaze didn't waver. "Then I suggest you mind your business," he said pointedly.

"Are you threatening me?" I could feel myself perspiring.

"Not at all," he said with a perfunctory smile. "Merely warning you."

I hurried past him and returned to the table. My stomach felt queasy. By now the talk had turned to soccer, thank goodness. I was happy to sit and listen without participating. Dessert was served—rich, dark chocolate mousse topped with whipped cream. In a moment Marcel returned to the table but said nothing.

"Where are you shopping for your store?" Renata asked as she poured coffee and passed the cups around.

I told her about my successes at Village Saint-Paul and mentioned that I might also have time for a trip to Luc's farm. Talk again turned to vegetables, with a heartfelt debate ensuing over what combination of seasonings constituted the most authentic herbes de Provence. At about midnight, Luc and I took our leave.

I started to hail a taxi, but Luc said, "Let's walk. It's a nice night." He linked his arm through mine, and we strolled through the darkened streets in comfortable silence. As we got to the Pont Neuf, we paused to gaze at the river. "I said too much, didn't I?" I said.

"You were very brave," he said, putting his arm around me. I leaned my head on his shoulder. "But being less brave might be wiser, no?"

"I suppose you're right," I said with a laugh.

We stood watching a lighted barge glide through the inky blackness of the river. I wanted to turn and kiss him. As I debated, he dropped his arm and said, "We'd better go." The moment was gone.

CHAPTER 26

After breakfast the next morning, I phoned Peter. "I'm making great progress," I told him excitedly, no longer maintaining any pretense that I was not pursuing Thalia's killer. "Guess what I found out? I'm pretty sure Marcel is involved in the illegal ivory trade!" I recounted how I'd followed him and snatched the envelope.

I was gratified by Peter's reaction. "You're on fire! Nicely done," he said. "Oh, I almost forgot. Detective Hernandez called again. He said he has a few more questions. I'm pretty sure he doesn't think Fred Gibson is the murderer."

"That's great!" I said. "Unless he's back to thinking it's me. I need to tell him what I found out about Marcel."

"He wants you to call him right away." We said goodbye, with a promise to talk tomorrow.

Next I took the Métro to Hôtel Sainte Bernadette. An attractive woman in her twenties was at the front desk. "Good morning," I said. "I called earlier about picking up a photo."

"Oh, yes, I have it right here for you." She retrieved the photo from behind the desk and handed it to me, saying earnestly, "I'm so sorry to learn about Madame Holcombe. No one here recalled seeing this man. We asked the whole staff. I do hope you're able to find him."

I thanked her and slipped the photo into my purse. As I turned to leave, she said, "I only remember one note being delivered for Madame Holcombe."

"Oh, when was that?"

"The last night that she stayed here. In August, I believe it was."

I felt a shiver of excitement. "Did you see the person who left it?"

"Yes, madame."

I took the photo of Marcel back out and laid it on the counter. "And you're sure it wasn't this man?"

"Oh, no," the clerk laughed. "It was a woman. I remember her very well. She wore a large diamond ring. And too much perfume."

"By any chance was it Chanel No. 5?"

"Um, yes." The young woman blushed and averted her eyes. "*Mille pardons.* I didn't realize she was a friend of yours."

"No need to apologize," I assured her. "You've been a great help." My thoughts were swirling. What the hell? Were Renata and Marcel in this together somehow? Had Thalia's killer served me boeuf bourguignon yesterday evening?

"I can't believe Thalia is gone," Tilly said as she poured tea into two Limoges cups. "She was so very full of life."

I'd met Tilly years ago when she ran an antiques business in the Tenth Arrondissement. Now she was retired. We'd remained friends, and I tried to visit whenever I was in Paris. It was a pleasure to sit in her sunny apartment and gaze out at the canal Saint-Martin. "After our tea, we'll take a walk," Tilly said. Like many Parisians, she walked several miles a day. No wonder she was still slim and spry at age seventy-three.

"Tilly, I want to show you something." I took the figurine from my handbag and held it out to her. She took it in her hand and turned it over. She examined it for several minutes, then said, "This is ivory. And judging from the style of carving, I would say it's new. That means it's very likely illegal."

"That's what I thought." I explained what I could about Marcel and the note he'd left at Arts de l'Orient, omitting any mention of his possible role in Thalia's death.

"You should report it. Let the police investigate."

"Yes, I probably should." I knew she was right. But I wasn't ready to involve the authorities yet. I didn't want to drag Etienne's company through an investigation if the only culprit was Marcel.

"Come, let's have our walk," Tilly said when we'd finished our tea. We strolled in the bright sunshine along the tree-lined canal. Bicyclists were out in full force, as were a few hardy souls sitting on the canal's edge with their bare feet dangling over. "What will you do now that Thalia's gone, *chérie*? Will you keep the shop going?"

"I'm not sure," I admitted. "My husband is urging a move, for his business. I may go with him."

"I see." She was silent for a moment. "You don't sound too happy about that."

"No, you're right. I love the house we live in, and I love our neighborhood. I have no desire to be anywhere else. As for the shop . . ."

"Yes?"

"Well, I hate to sound disloyal to Thalia, but I'm actually enjoying running it myself."

"That's perfectly understandable, my dear. Thalia had—how to say it—a strong personality."

We walked for about an hour, then turned back toward her apartment. As we were crossing the iron footbridge to her side of the street, I found myself wishing that Peter had suggested a move to Paris. *That* I would do in a heartbeat.

Back at her apartment, Tilly handed me a parcel. "Just a little something for your shop. I know how much you like Quimper." She'd affixed a rope around the box to serve as a carrying handle for the plane ride back. "And here's a roll of tape to take with you in case customs makes you open the box." She thought of everything.

Before saying goodbye, I urged her to visit me in California. "You know you're always welcome at my house," I said. She promised to think about it.

Making my way back toward the République Métro stop, I stood at a corner, waiting for the light to turn green. Just as I stepped off the curb, I heard someone shout, "*Regardez!*" and felt a hand gripping my arm, pulling me back onto the sidewalk. I stumbled and crashed to the ground as a black car sped through the intersection. I must have hit my head on the sidewalk because I had a ferocious pain in my right temple. People were crowded around me. Someone retrieved my precious package of Quimper plates. I hoped they weren't broken. I tried to get to my feet but sagged back to the ground. People were shouting all around me. "That driver was aiming for her," a woman in a red coat was insisting to the crowd. "He was looking right at her."

I closed my eyes, hoping that the dizziness would pass. Within minutes, an ambulance arrived, followed by the police. The woman in red immediately approached the gendarmes, undeterred when they tried to keep her back. "I'm a witness," she insisted loudly. "That driver deliberately tried to run this woman over." That got their attention. There were several other people eager to give a statement and describe the car, for which I was grateful.

Meanwhile I was on a gurney being carried into the ambulance. I called out to the man who had pulled me back. "Thank you. Thank you for saving my life."

He tipped his hat at me.

CHAPTER 27

The ambulance whisked me to Hôpital Saint-Louis. After looking me over, the admitting nurse told me that nothing seemed broken but they'd need to do X-rays to be certain. They wheeled me to the radiology department. I phoned Julien while I waited my turn. After assuring him I was fine, I asked what happened with Marie Resnais.

"I showed up at her office and waited outside at lunchtime. When she came out, I pretended to bump into her. She didn't remember me at first, but when I told her how I knew her, she acted friendly but definitely looked uncomfortable." He went on to tell me that he'd made idle conversation, then asked about her sick aunt in Dijon. "I said, 'I guess she's better now, since you're back.' She nodded and then hurried away."

"Well, maybe it was legitimate."

"No! Don't you remember? She told us it was her grandmother who was sick! She's lying. Somehow Marcel got her to leave so he could take her place."

I had to admit his theory was making sense. "If you can, take a look at Marcel's job application and see where he worked before—or where he says he worked. Text me."

Within five minutes, Julien texted me back with the name

and number of Marcel's previous employer. I phoned them. "Good afternoon. I'm calling to check on a reference for a former employee of yours, Marcel Benoit." The receptionist didn't know the name but admitted she was fairly new. She connected me to a man who also was unfamiliar with Marcel. "What department did he work in, madam?"

"Um, well the job I'm considering him for is handling imports from Africa."

I was put on hold for some time, until finally a man came on who did know Marcel, much to my disappointment. "Yes, we were sorry to lose him after two decades. He retired." I thanked him and hung up as a hospital attendant approached.

He wheeled me into another room, where they took numerous X-rays. Then I was parked in a waiting room and assured that the radiologist would examine the film very soon. I sighed. More waiting. I called Peter. Naturally, he was alarmed to hear about my accident. He even offered to catch the next flight to Paris. "That's very sweet but absolutely unnecessary. I'm just a little bruised," I told him. He tried to convince me to cut my trip short, but I assured him again that I was perfectly fine. "Nothing to worry about. I'm waiting for them to give me the all clear so I can go back to my hotel."

As soon as we said goodbye, I vomited all over myself. That created a flurry of activity in the room. As one nurse was helping me into a clean gown, a young doctor came in, shined a flashlight in each eye, and concluded I had a mild concussion.

"So am I supposed to go home and rest?"

"No, you'll need to spend the night here. We want to check you again in the morning."

Damn. The good news, though, was that the X-rays showed nothing was broken. I was wheeled up to a sunny room on the third floor. What a time to be stuck in bed. My next phone call was to Luc. I told him about Julien's encounter with Marie Resnais and about Marcel's seemingly bogus work history. "No way could he have worked somewhere for decades," I said. "He looks like he's only in his thirties."

Luc agreed that something was fishy. While we were on the phone, a nurse came in to check my blood pressure. Luc said, "What's going on? Who were you talking to?"

"Oh, um, I'm in the hospital," I said. I grimaced as he scolded me in rapid French for not telling him right away. More scolding followed when I told him about the accident. "I'm fine. Nothing is broken." I omitted the detail about the concussion.

"Listen, if we're dealing with animal poachers—which it seems we are—killing means nothing to them. You could be putting your life in danger, Rae."

"No, no, it was an accident. Someone ran a red light. Luckily a man standing next to me pulled me back onto the curb."

"Thank goodness. I would never forgive myself if something happened to you." I didn't see how it could be his fault, but I appreciated his concern. I assured him again that I was fine.

"How about some company while you're stuck in the hospital?"

"Not today. I need to sleep. But if I'm still here tomorrow, definitely! See if you can find out more about the real Marcel." I gave him the name of the man I spoke with who said Marcel had retired. "Oh, I almost forgot. I have more news. It was Renata who brought the first note to Thalia."

"Really!"

I went on to tell him what I'd learned from the hotel clerk. We theorized for a while about what it all might mean. "So maybe the notes really were about the affair," I said. It seemed a little far-fetched that Renata would lure Thalia to the park to kill her. But, Luc pointed out, not if Etienne was planning to leave Renata. "People kill their spouses' mistresses all the time," he said. "And Thalia being pregnant might have sent her over the edge."

"True. But where would she get a gun? My gut tells me that Marcel is involved somehow. All his lies—he's not who he seems."

I had to end the phone call then because two police officers strode into my room, accompanied by a frowning nurse who told them they had only five minutes to speak to me. They agreed to be brief. They took down all the information I had, which wasn't much. I hadn't seen the driver's face, and all I remembered of the car was that it was black. I was certain I'd looked both ways before stepping off the curb and that the nearest car had been some distance away.

One officer showed me a sketch, based on the description by the woman in the red coat. "Do you recognize this man?"

I shook my head, which hurt like hell.

"Do you know of any reason that someone would want to injure you?"

"I . . . I don't know." Well, yes, I actually did. I seemed to be pursuing a ring of animal poachers. But I decided to say nothing about that. "I'm sorry, I don't know anything else except what I've told you."

"*Bien.* We have a description of the car, along with conflicting reports of the license number. We're still searching." They promised to call me when they had more information.

That night, I slept fitfully, dreaming about Marcel slaughtering elephants while Renata showed me her extensive diamond collection.

Early the next morning, a neurologist came in to examine me. After having me parade around the room, touch my nose, stand on one foot, and perform other acrobatics, he pronounced me fit to go. I walked out into a crisp autumn morning and was helped into a taxi. Luc had offered to pick me up, but with my swollen face, I wasn't eager to see him right now.

The hotel clerk made a huge fuss over me when I showed up limping and bruised. He insisted on riding in the elevator with me and helping me into bed. "Madame Sullivan, do not hesitate to ring if there's anything at all you need."

I thanked him and popped a few pain pills. As soon as I lay down, my phone rang. I saw that it was that awful reporter Barbara Abrams. Naturally, I didn't answer.

CHAPTER 28

The next day, the hotel clerk had breakfast brought up to my room, for which I was grateful. I was even more sore than the previous day, with ugly purple bruises on my left arm and my temple. I was buttering my toast when Sonia phoned.

"Are you OK? Peter told me you were in an accident. Why in the world didn't you call me?"

"Oh, it's nothing. Really. How are things there?"

"Are you actually fine, or are you just saying that?" she demanded. It took a while, but she was finally satisfied that I was OK. "Joe and I went out for coffee," she said.

"Who?"

"Detective Levine."

"I thought you couldn't date until the investigation is over."

"It wasn't a date. Well, not really. He asked me some questions about Thalia. So that makes it an interview, right? Actually, I could tell he was really reaching to come up with anything to ask. So I guess it was a date." She sounded happy.

"Did he say anything about the case?"

"Not much. He can't really talk about it. Fred Gibson has been charged with being in possession of stolen property. Not murder."

"So they don't believe he did it?"

"I'm not sure what they believe. But they don't have enough evidence tying him to the murder. There were only a few tiny spots of Thalia's blood on his clothes. And Joe said those clothes hadn't been washed since the Clinton administration."

I laughed. "What about Garrett? Are they still hounding him?"

"Joe hasn't said anything about that. He did tell me that Hernandez has been putting in extra hours working the case," Sonia said. "He's due to retire in a month, and he's determined to nail the killer before he goes. Oh, and he was *not* happy to find out you went to France. I told him you had to go for business and that you'd be back in ten days."

We talked for a while longer, then I hung up and returned to my breakfast. My phone rang again. It was Luc.

"You were right!" he told me. "Marcel is not who he says he is. The man who retired, the real Marcel Benoit, was sixty-two years old."

"I knew he was a fake! And somehow he convinced or bribed Marie to leave her job and recommend him."

"You haven't heard the best part yet," Luc said. "My friend at the Val-de-Marne Préfecture did some digging about Etienne's company. She didn't find any dirt on the business. But two years ago a restraining order was filed against Renata Duchamp by someone named Laurette Girard."

"Who is she?"

"Apparently, Etienne was having an affair with her at the time. Renata began harassing her, sending threatening letters, phoning her at all hours."

So what did this all mean? Luc and I batted around some ideas, but we couldn't come up with a cohesive theory. Were Marcel and

Renata in it together? Was the blackmail just a ruse to lure Thalia to her death? If so, why wasn't she killed right away at six thirty? We had no answers, just lots of questions. "So what's our next move?" I asked.

"Your next move, my sweet, is to come to the farm with me. I need to get back to work, and you need to get out of Paris before any more motorists try to run you down. We're taking the train tomorrow morning. I'll pick you up in a taxi at eight thirty. Be ready."

A trip to the farm sounded wonderful. But I felt a twinge of guilt. Shouldn't I be pursuing Thalia's killer, rather than having a holiday with Luc? Not to mention the fact that I was married.

The next morning, Luc and I puzzled further over the revelations about Renata as we sat sipping coffee at a café in the station. "It doesn't make sense," he said. "Why would she blackmail my sister? She doesn't need money." Neither of us spoke for a few minutes. Then Luc said, "Do you think Renata is somehow involved in the smuggling?"

"Maybe. I spent hours online before bed last night, reading about the ivory trade. It's heartbreaking. How can people be so evil?"

He reached out a hand and put it over mine. "Come on, we have a train to catch," he said.

Our train pulled out of Gare du Nord right on time, traveling slowly through the Tenth Arrondissement and then the grimy outskirts of the city. Luc read the newspaper as I looked out the window. Dreary tenements marred the view, the same kind of thoughtlessly designed housing that blighted big cities back home. Graffiti was everywhere along the walls bordering the train tracks. We crossed into morose-looking suburbs filled with more of the same grim-looking housing. "This is where the riots were in 2005," Luc said. "People set cars on fire." After about fifteen minutes, the landscape became less urban. The houses were smaller and modest, but at least there was some green space around them. I leaned back and closed my eyes, hovering on the verge of sleep. When I opened my eyes again, the landscape had given way to flat fields. Every so often we passed a group of cows munching grass. "We're nearly there," Luc said.

We alighted in the pretty town of Chantilly, then walked uphill to where Luc had parked his truck. It was a half hour drive from here to the tiny village where his farm was located. The narrow main street was lined with stone buildings, their facades burnished to a golden patina by decades of sun and storms. There was a small grocery shop, a post office, a butcher shop, and a bakery on one side of the street. Opposite was a barn-like store that sold animal feed and other farm supplies. Carved over its front door was the original blacksmith's sign. I stood trans-fixed at this town that looked frozen in time. As the noise of the train faded in the distance, a deep quiet filled the space, punctu-ated only by birdsong. But it was the earthy scent in the air that made me swoon. "What's that smell?" I asked Luc.

"What smell?" he asked, hoisting our bags and crossing the street.

I followed. "Don't you smell it?" I asked incredulously.

"Nope." Luc stopped at an old pickup truck, once red but now faded to a dusty brown. He tossed the bags in the back. "Probably the grass. It's hay season. Come on. I need to check the mail." Leaving the bags sitting in plain sight in the open bed of the truck, we walked down the block to the post office.

Luc introduced me to the postmaster, a wiry old man who tipped his tweed cap at me. The man handed Luc a bundle of letters and a package, then asked him about eggs. Luc promised to deliver a basketful tomorrow. The old man tipped his hat again as we left. Luc opened the passenger door of the truck for me. It wasn't locked.

We drove a couple of miles down a narrow lane, lush with fennel growing wild on either side. The heady aroma was even more pronounced now, a mixture at once sweet, musky, and spicy, like some divine elixir of the gods. We passed a man pedaling a bicycle, a large basket on his back, with thick leather straps over his shoulders. He waved at Luc. We turned off onto a dirt road and drove another mile or two. I sat gulping the fragrant air, intoxicated by nature's redolence. I looked at Luc, so comfortable in his element. Sensing my gaze, he turned toward me and smiled. "You like it here," he said. It wasn't a question. I nodded, deliriously happy. "I knew you would," he said.

Eventually we turned into a gravel driveway and pulled up in front of a two-story stone house. A plump woman wearing a white apron over her navy dress came down the front steps. "Bonjour, monsieur Luc. Welcome back." As soon as Luc emerged from the truck, she kissed him on both cheeks.

Luc introduced me. "This is Madame P. She runs the place. Couldn't do a thing without her."

"Oh, don't talk such nonsense," Madame P. said, but she was clearly pleased. She made a big fuss over me. "Imagine coming all this way from California!" She made it sound as if I'd undertaken a perilous journey. After being assured that I was neither hungry nor thirsty, Madame P. showed me to my room on the second floor under the eaves. It was perfect in every detail. Its sloping ceiling was low, as was typical in a house built two hundred years ago when people were a good deal smaller. The high bed was covered in a hand-sewn quilt. Filmy white curtains hung over the leaded glass window, which had a panoramic view of the fields behind the house. An armload of fresh lavender stood in a glass jar on the painted white dresser, perfuming the air. "I hope this suits you, dear. Monsieur Luc said he had a very special guest coming. Well, I'll leave you to unpack."

I washed my face at the small porcelain sink in the corner, brushed my hair, and decided that unpacking could wait. Before descending the stairs, I peeked into Luc's bedroom. It was a little larger than mine and had a similar leaded glass window, but without curtains. The big iron bed nearly filled the space. Stacks of books were piled on the whitewashed floor. A reading lamp was on a small table to the left of the bed. No lamp on the right, I noted. Maybe that meant he never had overnight company. Or, more likely, when he did, reading was not a priority. I went downstairs.

"Ready for the tour?" Luc asked. "Oh, these are for you." He handed me two small brown envelopes. "Seeds from last year's sucrine lettuce crop," he said. "It's a favorite around here." I tucked the packets in my pocket and followed him through the grounds almost reverently, feeling I was being afforded a glimpse of paradise that at any moment might be snatched away. It was all so . . . so . . . *alive* was the word that came to mind. Raised beds were bursting with voluptuous cabbages, red-veined chard, and moist-leaved kale. Pole beans covered trellises in flowery cascades. Borage, mint, sage, and lavender spilled over the edges of beds and onto the paths. A small crew of workers went about the business of watering and weeding, their rubber boots crunching on the gravel. Luc led me to the orchards, where leafy apple, peach, and pomegranate trees hung heavy with fruit. Birdsong filled the air. The flower gardens brimmed with huge drifts, and every turn in the path revealed another treasure: butterflies hovering over a wide bowl of water set on a rock, a tiny chair and table tucked under the shade of towering clematis, a tumbledown shed with grapevines scrambling over the top. Every so often we came upon another plump cat sunning itself. I had never seen anything quite this wonderful.

Next was the chicken pen, which was the size of my entire backyard at home. A flock of about two dozen hens gathered around Luc's feet expectantly, parting as he walked among them. "Sorry, ladies, you already ate," Luc told them. He unhooked two baskets hanging on the fence and gave one to me. "Come," he said, "let's gather some eggs. I'll cook you an omelet for dinner." We entered the coop, and Luc showed me how to reach into the nesting boxes and feel under the straw. I found two still-warm eggs and held them in my hand, marveling at their perfection. I had the irrational urge to take them home and display them. Eating them seemed irreverent somehow.

Luc showed me the beehives, sited amid drifts of lavender. "It gives the honey an incredible flavor," he explained. "Did you know that bees visit about two million flowers to produce a pound of honey?" Nothing surprised me at this point. The very act of eating now seemed profound, a celebration of the miracle of nature. Did Luc feel that way too? I wondered. Or was he just so used to all this glory?

Luc saved the best for last. "The pigs!" I exclaimed with delight. There were three of them, nosing one another out of the way to be scratched. "This is Belle, this is Jolie, and this is Madeleine," Luc said.

"Are they babies?"

"No, they're full-grown. This is as big as they get. They're just for fun. No bacon," he assured me. I peered into their little wooden house, carpeted with a thick layer of straw. "They get chilly at night," Luc said. "They're originally from Vietnam, so they like it tropical. When it gets really cold, I put a heat lamp in here."

We eventually made our way back to the house, where Madame P. announced lunch. The dining room table was set with a linen cloth. "Very fancy," Luc said, smiling. "I usually eat lunch sitting on the front steps." Lunch was a soup brimming with homegrown vegetables and herbs, plus thick slices of hearty homemade bread. When we finished, Luc said, "I have some work to do. Feel free to take a nap or explore. There's a bicycle behind the shed. I'll see you at dinner."

"It's very good that you're here," Madame P. said as she and I washed the lunch dishes. "Monsieur Luc never has visitors. A young handsome man like that. Such a shame that all he cares about is the farm." She shook her head in disapproval. "He works too hard. I tell him all the time, 'You should hire more help.' Well, at least now he'll have some money, now that his sister died. He wants to expand."

"Oh?"

"The parcel adjacent to this is for sale. The man who lives there is too old to farm any longer. He's going off to live with his son. Monsieur Luc was hoping to sell a building in Amiens that he owned with his sister. He wanted to use the money to buy the land. But his sister said no."

I recalled Thalia mentioning this.

"That's why he went to see her," Madame P. continued. "He hoped to convince her. Of course, now that she has died"—here she crossed herself—"the property in Amiens belongs to him. He's already put it up for sale. He's determined to buy that property down the road."

I mulled over this information. Well, sad as Thalia's death was, at least Luc could now have the land he wanted.

"You know he and his sister didn't speak for years," Madame P. went on. "Some silly nonsense about his father's will. It seems the old man left everything to Thalia—his stepdaughter by his second wife. Can you imagine disinheriting your own flesh and blood? Not that Thalia wasn't a lovely girl." She crossed herself again. "And I can't really say I blame the man. Young Luc went through a low period. Of course, it wasn't his fault. He fell in with a bad crowd. And look at how wonderful he turned out in the end. If only his father had lived to see it."

"Oh, yes. He's certainly wonderful." I was eager to know more about this "low period," but I didn't ask. After the dishes were dried and put away, I went up to my room and changed my shoes. Then I wheeled the bike out from behind the shed and pedaled off. I was still sore and bruised, but I couldn't resist exploring. I turned left at the end of the driveway, continuing farther on the road we had come in on. What if I never left this magical place? I wondered. What if I stayed here and became stepmother to Belle, Jolie, and Madeleine? I would grow flowers and zucchinis. And paint pictures. Jasper could be sent for. He'd adore it here. Of course, I'd have to teach him not to chase the cats.

I groaned out loud. I was married. To a wonderful man who loved me. And here I was making plans to be Luc's new room-mate. Maybe Peter and I *should* go to Arizona. A change would be good. I could grow zucchinis there and keep bees. But the problem was, I realized, I didn't want to be a beekeeper with Peter because he would consider it a waste of time when you could just buy honey at the grocery store. Of course, that was no reason to not stay married to someone, I reminded myself, engrossed now in my internal dialogue. If an interest in keeping bees was a requirement for marriage, most men would be single. Women too, for that matter. You're being silly, I told myself.

But the pull of this place was potent. It spoke to me in a way I couldn't explain, as if I'd always been meant to be here.

I pedaled for hours, then returned to the farm at dusk, weary and content. Luc was still out in the field, talking with one of the workers. I went up to my room and read until I heard Luc in the kitchen. I went downstairs and offered to help, but he shooed me out, so I went back to my book until dinnertime.

Luc had prepared a fluffy omelet filled with sautéed wild mushrooms. "Oh my God, this is incredible," I said at the first bite.

"Fresh eggs," he said. "There's nothing like them."

There was salad with shaved fennel, more of that amazing homemade bread, and wine. Lots of wine. I could be very happy here. I imagined how it would feel to go upstairs and climb into that big iron bed. With Luc.

"Well, I'd better head upstairs," Luc said, interrupting my thoughts. "I need to be up early. No more lounging around like in the city." He walked over to my chair and kissed me on the forehead. "*Bonsoir*," he said. "Do you have everything you need?"

"Yes, everything is perfect."

CHAPTER 29

A panicky phone call from Julien at seven in the morning altered my plans to spend the day exploring Chantilly. "We're leaving for Marseille today," he said urgently. "I don't know why, but Jerome changed the schedule. And Marcel tried to keep me from going, so I'm sure there's something important happening."

"We'd better go today, too," Luc said when I told him. "We can drive. It's long—seven hours—but this way we can leave immediately instead of going to Paris first and changing trains." We hurriedly packed our bags, downed some coffee, and were on the road in Luc's Peugeot.

At his suggestion, I took the wheel so he could phone the hotel and revise our reservation. Unfortunately, the place was completely booked for the night. As we headed south, he made call after call in an attempt to locate available rooms on short notice.

This was it, I told myself. Finally, we were on the way to expose Marcel. We'd catch him red-handed receiving whatever illicit merchandise was arriving from Africa. And then the police—even Detective Hernandez—would have to suspect him of murder. I suddenly remembered that I was supposed to call him, but I wasn't about to stop now. I could talk to him once we reached Marseille.

"OK, I finally found a place," Luc announced as he put his phone in his pocket. "It's not in a good section of town, though. But it's only for tonight. Tomorrow we'll move."

"That's fine," I said.

"And it only has one double bed. I hope that's OK with you."

"Sure." I tried to sound as casual as if he'd just told me the hotel didn't offer breakfast, but my voice had a strangled quality. I drove in silence, forcing myself to think about Renata—any topic other than the prospect of climbing into bed with Luc. How was she connected with Marcel? And why was she blackmailing Thalia? I couldn't come up with any satisfactory explanation.

After several hours, we stopped to fill the gas tank and eat a quick lunch, then Luc took over the driving for the remainder of the trip. The sun was directly overhead now, and the interior of the car was roasting hot. Opening the windows at least created a breeze, but the air was heavy with heat. I was developing a fierce headache.

We finally pulled into Marseille at four thirty. Even at this hour, the heat was still palpable. As Luc had warned, our hotel was in a seedy neighborhood, the buildings covered in graffiti and the alleyways lined with overflowing trash cans. A smell of fish hung in the air. At least we weren't far from the waterfront, which was where we'd need to meet Julien.

My headache was in full force as we entered the dingy lobby, one bare light bulb hanging down over the front desk. The man behind it smelled of alcohol and sweat. An electric fan was pointed at him, which only served to spread the odor throughout the lobby. Luc checked us in, while the man ogled me. "Enjoy yourselves," he said. "We are very discreet here." I glared at him, which only seemed to amuse him. "Stairs are through that door," he said, inclining his head. "Elevator is broken."

We lugged our bags upstairs. The room smelled musty, but at least it looked reasonably clean. The lone window faced tall, gray buildings across an alley. I pulled the curtains closed, unpacked my aspirin, and swallowed three.

Luc went into the bathroom to get cleaned up. I lay back against the pillow and closed my eyes. It was too hot to even think. My mind drifted, until the sound of Luc's ringing phone startled me. I made a move to answer it, but Luc beat me to it, dashing out of the bathroom with a towel around his waist. "*Allô? Oui. Nous sommes arrivés. À l'hôtel.*" He turned to me. "It's Julien. Do you have a piece of paper?"

I got paper and pen from my bag, feeling flustered at Luc's half-naked presence. His torso was hard and rippled from all that manual labor. Luc scribbled on the paper, then hung up. "I have directions to the warehouse. We're going to meet him in the morning. He'll call us."

"Sounds good."

"Let's relax tonight. Have a nice dinner. There's a seafood place I want to take you to."

A long, cool shower and an evening out with no talk of murder was just what I needed.

We drove into Old Port and walked the cobblestone streets. Luc took me to his favorite *fromagerie*, where we sampled half a dozen cheeses and bought a crock of creamy Saint-Marcellin. Then we ate mussels at a café overlooking the Mediterranean. By the time we returned to the hotel, I was reinvigorated and my headache was long gone.

"So what's the plan for tomorrow?" I asked. "What exactly will we do when we find out what Marcel is up to?"

"We'll go to the police and tell them everything. And Julien will tell his father, of course. Then we're finished. We'll let the authorities handle it." I nodded in agreement. After a minute, he asked, "Do you think Etienne is involved?"

I sighed. "I don't know. I hope not. I'd like to think that Thalia wouldn't have fallen for a criminal. She was pretty sharp."

"True. But she didn't really spend a lot of time with him. He could have easily kept his illegal dealings hidden."

"I guess." It seemed to me that if you were sleeping with someone, you'd have insight into his ethics. But maybe I was being naive. After all, Etienne was cheating on his wife, so how ethical was he, really? "I'm going to get ready for bed," I announced.

I took my bag into the bathroom, wondering what the correct attire would be for sharing a bed with a man who was not my husband. I finally settled on stretchy yoga pants and a tank top. The outfit highlighted everything nicely, yet I was covered up. Let him figure out what I wanted. I sure as hell couldn't decide. I washed my face and brushed my teeth. When I came out of the bathroom, Luc was sitting up in bed under the covers. His bedside light was on, and he was reading the newspaper. He was shirtless again. Was he naked under the covers?

"Will it bother you if I read for a while?" he asked.

"No, not at all." I took a book out of my bag and got into bed cautiously, being scrupulous about staying on my side. I read until my eyes were heavy. Finally I turned out the lamp on my side. Was he going to read the paper all damn night? Within minutes, I was asleep. I don't know when Luc finally turned out the light, but it was dark when I was awakened by the ringing of a phone.

"Hello?" Luc said sleepily. I could hear Julien's agitated voice on the other end but couldn't make out what he was saying. "Here, talk to Rae. We're leaving now."

He handed me the phone, got out of bed—turns out he was naked—and threw on his clothes. He motioned to me to get up. Julien was hissing in my ear. "Marcel got up during the night and left. I followed him. I'm in a taxi. Please come right away."

"Yes. Yes, we're coming." I grabbed my purse, slipped on my shoes, and we were out the door.

CHAPTER 30

s Luc drove through the narrow, twisting streets toward the waterfront, I navigated, peering at the map while talking to Julien on speakerphone. "Keep going south," I said. "Toward the water. I haven't found the street yet. Camargue, de Gaulle . . . here it is! OK, go right."

The streets were dimly lit. A few bars were open, their neon signs casting shimmering reflections on the fog-damp sidewalks. At the next corner, two women wearing miniskirts and thigh-high boots were smoking cigarettes.

"OK, your left turn is coming up. Shit. I can't read the street signs. It should be the next one." I was able to make out the sign just as we were driving past the turn. "That's it! Sorry. OK, circle around and go back." At last we caught sight of the cab. The waterfront was two blocks ahead of us now. A thin mist drifted off the water and swirled around the buildings.

Luc grabbed the phone out of my hand. "We see you. Pay the fare and get out," he told Julien. We stopped twenty feet behind the cab and waited. In a moment, Julien got out and ran toward our car. He jumped into the back seat. "I'm sure they went to the warehouse. It's really close to here, straight ahead," he said breathlessly. "The gates will be locked, but I saw a hole in the fence when I was there this afternoon."

As we pulled up along the waterfront, Julien said, "That's Jerome's car. They're here. Park." The shiny black car was inside the chain-link fence, along with several vans. There wasn't anyone in sight. We all got out of the car and stood there for a moment, looking at the two-story warehouse. Foghorns sounded faintly in the distance.

Julien found the spot in the fence where the chain link was loose. He rolled it back, and we scrambled through just as lights came on in the first-floor windows. Then, after a few moments, more lights came on in a small window upstairs. "That's an office up there," Julien said. "I was in there yesterday. Downstairs are all the shipments, still in containers. Listen, I'll go up the fire escape and take a look through the window."

"Wait!" Luc said, but Julien had already broken into a run across the parking lot. We watched helplessly as he got to the bottom of the ladder, which hung five feet above him. He lugged some wooden pallets in place beneath, stood on them, and grabbed hold of the bottom rung. Then he hoisted himself and quickly scaled the ladder to the fire escape one floor above. Keeping close to the wall of the building, he inched along toward the lighted window and peered in.

My heart was beating fast. "Come on, come on," I muttered. Apparently Julien had seen enough. He turned and made his way back toward the ladder. I exhaled with relief. But suddenly the window opened, and a figure stepped out onto the fire escape. It was Marcel. I gasped and Luc clapped a hand over my mouth, pulling me down into a crouch in the shadows. I watched in horror as Julien spun around and froze. Then Marcel grasped his arm and climbed back inside the window, pulling Julien along with him. The window closed.

Almost simultaneously, the massive warehouse door rolled up and five men came out of the building. They opened the backs of both vans. They were getting ready to load the goods.

"Oh my God," I said, "they've got Julien."

"I'm going in to get him," Luc said in a determined voice. "Call the police. Here." He pushed his phone into my hand. "Dial one-seven. Then get back in the car as fast as you can and lock the doors."

"Luc, don't leave me out here."

"You'll be safe in the car."

"Luc, be careful—"

"Dial!" he commanded.

I dialed the phone, speaking to the operator in French. All the while my eyes were on Luc. The five men had gone back inside. Luc approached the building, looked around stealthily, then walked through the open roll-up door, vanishing from my view. "Yes, Pier Thirty-three. Please hurry!"

I hung up and ran back to the car. After a few minutes, there was still no sign of the police. I could stay here and wait, or I could go find Julien and Luc. Dammit. I wasn't going to just sit and do nothing. I left the car and hurried back to the warehouse, where the door was still rolled up. I slipped inside, into the blackness. Luc had taken the flashlight, not that I'd dare turn it on anyway even if I had it.

I felt my way along the wall, navigating around objects. Dim light from streetlamps streamed in behind me from the open door. After a few moments, I could make out shapes better, and I moved forward with more confidence. This cavernous warehouse had no sound of voices, but I could hear footsteps overhead. I pressed forward, not knowing where I was headed but determined to find Julien. At last I saw a set of stairs. I tiptoed up a long flight and opened the door at the top. The light was bright. I gasped.

There were three men rifling through files. And in a corner was Luc, bound and gagged, sitting in a chair. One of the men whirled around to face me. It was Jerome. At first I felt a wave of relief. Then I realized he was pointing a gun at my stomach. "Get in here," he growled. He grabbed my arm roughly and shoved me into a chair, then bound my hands with duct tape.

"Where's Julien?" I demanded. "What have you done with Julien?"

"He's at the hotel behaving himself. Like you should have done," said Jerome. "Too bad my driver in Paris had such poor aim. You weren't supposed to recover from that little road accident." He shoved a rag in my mouth. "This will shut you up."

Starting to gag on the dirty rag pressing on my tongue, I forced myself to take deep breaths. I couldn't pass out. I had to find Julien. I looked over at Luc. He gave a little nod, as if to say, You're OK. Breathe, breathe, I told myself. I wondered whether Jerome was going to leave us here. Would we survive until someone found us? How long would it be? I felt rising panic.

"Go and start loading," Jerome said. The men turned to leave the room. "Remember," Jerome called out, "Ivory on the bottom, then the textiles on top, in case anyone searches the van." He turned back toward us prisoners and smiled sadistically. "Now, what to do with you two meddlers. I hate to get the office all bloody. I suppose I'll have to take you outside to kill you." He looked at Luc. "We'll start with you, I think." He slipped the gun into his jacket pocket and approached Luc. "I'm going to untie you from the chair. If you cause any trouble, I'll shoot her immediately. Do you understand?"

Luc nodded. Jerome went around behind Luc and started to loosen the straps securing him to the chair. I wondered if I could drag my chair over and knock him down. My heart lurched when I saw Marcel standing in the doorway holding a pistol. "Step away from the chair," he said.

Jerome looked up. "What the hell are you doing?"

"Step away from the chair, I said."

A look of resignation crossed Jerome's face. He started to move away from Luc's chair, then with lightning speed pulled the gun out of his pocket and pointed it at Marcel. I screamed, but the gag reduced it to a choking sound. They both fired, and Jerome fell to the ground, silent. Quickly Marcel went to the limp body and pocketed the gun. He felt for a pulse, then nodded. "He's still alive," he said. Then Marcel removed our gags. "You must remain quiet. Do you understand? Not a word." Luc and I nodded.

I wanted to ask him about Julien, but I sat in frozen silence. Were we rescued or were we about to be murdered? I wasn't sure. I heard sirens approaching. "You called the police, didn't you?" Marcel asked. Luc nodded. "OK. It will be OK. Not what I was planning on, but I have enough evidence."

I had a million questions. Nothing made sense. But that was becoming the norm in the last few months since I'd fallen down the rabbit hole of murder.

"I've been after these guys for some time. And you almost screwed it up," Marcel scolded. He admonished us again not to make a sound before leaving the room.

My memory of what happened next is a bit jumbled. There was a lot of shouting, noise, some gunfire, sirens. Maybe not in that order. People running up the stairs. The lights came on, and a uniformed policeman untied me and Luc and led us down the stairs and outside to a patrol car. Julien was already ensconced in the back seat. "Wasn't that spectacular?" he said, wide-eyed. "Too bad Jerome got shot, of course, but it's his own fault." He talked nonstop during the ride to the police station, clearly in shock. Luc sat in the middle, with one arm around each of us.

We sipped horrid coffee at the police station. I couldn't stop shivering, even though someone had put a jacket around my shoulders. The questions went on for hours, it seemed. Explaining why we were there, how we were connected with Jerome, with Etienne's company. I kept trying to explain about Thalia, but nobody seemed interested in her.

Marcel came in, his arm in a sling. For the first time ever, I was actually happy to see him. I begged him to explain what was going on.

"I'll tell you this much. Jerome has been smuggling ivory for years. We've been closing in on him. He was doing it through the company."

"Did Etienne know?"

"No. We thought so at first. The company had suspicious dealings. I was placed there undercover. We paid an employee to go on leave, and I took her place. But I soon figured out—"

"You're a police officer?" I interrupted.

"Not exactly. I work for the European Union." He continued, "I soon realized Jerome was operating without Etienne's knowledge. Your friend Thalia caught me looking through the files. I'm afraid she got the wrong impression of me—as did young Julien. But, of course, I couldn't confide in her. I couldn't jeopardize the operation."

"So . . . so you killed her?" I asked incredulously.

"What? No!" He looked appalled. "Of course not."

"But, then who . . . did Jerome kill her? Did she find out the truth about him?"

"That I don't know. Jerome has broken a lot of laws, that's for certain, but whether he killed your friend, I don't know."

Finally we were free to go. A police officer drove the three of us back to our hotel. Our arrival elicited a smirk from the desk clerk, but we ignored him and trudged upstairs. Luc insisted that Julien and I take the bed. He rolled up some clothes for a pillow and slept on the floor, covered in a jacket. I climbed into bed feeling a mix of gratitude at being alive and a profound sense of disappointment. "It's not Marcel," I said to myself over and over. I thought of calling Peter to let him know I was OK but realized that he had no idea I'd even been in danger. And I was too tired to talk to anyone.

The next morning I woke feeling new bruises. Sure enough, my cheek was swollen and blackened. My wrists were scraped from the rough rope. Julien and Luc were already up and dressed. Hardly a word was spoken by any of us as we packed up and started the long drive back to Paris. We only stopped once, for some coffee and a soda. We finally arrived at Julien's home in the early evening, exhausted and bedraggled. Julien unlocked the door to the apartment, and we followed him inside.

Both his parents came running to greet him. Etienne hugged the boy and kissed him, while Renata launched into a tirade. "What in the world were you thinking?" she said to him. "You could have been killed. Why didn't you call the police?" Julien tried to stem the flow, but she wouldn't listen. Then she turned her anger on me and Luc. "Him I could understand," she said, nodding at Julien. "But you two are adults. How could you be so foolhardy?"

"*Maman*, it was fun," Julien said.

"Not another word out of you," she said sternly to him. "Say goodbye and go to your room." Julien hugged us, then left the room. When he was out of earshot, Renata said with intensity to me, "Is it not enough that your friend carried on with my husband? Now, because of you, my son was nearly killed. Please leave my house." She strode out of the room.

Etienne said, "Thank you for bringing Julien home safely." As he walked us to the door, he said softly, "I should have treated her better."

I said nothing, and he continued. "Thalia told me she was pregnant and that I was the father. I'm afraid I didn't react the way she was hoping. She seemed to think we'd start a new life together with the baby. But that just wasn't possible for me." He spread both hands as if to say, How could I give up all this? "I suppose she talked to you about our disagreement."

"No, she never said anything. I had no idea she was pregnant."

He sighed. "She was a remarkable woman. Remarkable. The time I had with her is something that I'll always treasure." He looked close to tears, but I felt no sympathy for him. He'd never had any intention of leaving his family, but he'd led Thalia to believe otherwise.

As I turned to go, he put a hand on my arm. "I understand why you and Julien did what you did," he said. "You wanted justice for Thalia. I'm sorry it didn't turn out as you'd hoped." We said our goodbyes.

Luc drove to my hotel and parked the car. "Are you going back to the farm now?" I asked. "Not yet," he smiled at me. "Come, let's get some dinner. We haven't eaten all day." We walked to a corner bistro. I ordered some soup but couldn't eat more than a few sips. How had this all gone so wrong? I wondered. "I was a fool," I said. "What made me think I could solve Thalia's murder? Renata is right. I nearly got us all killed."

After dinner we walked through the streets of Paris, a gentle rain falling. When we got back to my hotel, Luc put his arms around me and kissed me. A real kiss. "Goodbye, Rae," he said softly. "Please come visit me again, under happier circumstances." I promised to do that. We kissed again. I went upstairs to my room, packed, and changed my flight home to the following day.

CHAPTER 31

I wallowed in self-loathing during much of the transatlantic flight. God, I'd made a mess of things. No wonder Detective Hernandez hadn't taken my rants about Marcel seriously. He must have learned at the very first interview that Marcel was a cop. That's probably why he wanted me to call him when he heard I was in France—to warn me to stay out of the wildlife poaching investigation. Well, I didn't need to call him back now. I was safe, and I certainly didn't want a lecture.

How had I been so colossally wrong? Marcel was one of the good guys. Jerome was a slime and maybe a killer. Renata . . . well, what exactly was Renata's role in all this? The note she'd left at Thalia's hotel made sense, given her history of stalking her husband's lovers. But I was stumped by the blackmail. And I was still stinging from her rebuke yesterday. She was right. I'd encouraged her son to put himself in danger. I should have simply gone to the police about the smuggling.

All the doubts I'd entertained right after the murder came flooding back. Not only was I a failure at sleuthing, but was I also deluding myself thinking I could operate the business without Thalia? She had been the driving force, it seemed, while I tagged along. Maybe I wasn't cut out to run the show. And look where my misguided efforts at detection had gotten me: bruised and humiliated. I had failed miserably. Then there was Peter. I'd been treating him like crap, caught up in a schoolgirl crush, running off to France.

I was passing over the Great Lakes when I made the mistake of reading the *Chronicle* article about me. I'd resisted for weeks, heeding Peter's advice to ignore it. Although the article adopted a pseudosympathetic tone, it did rehash the whole stolen-art debacle and subtly implied that it was no coincidence I was now connected with a murder investigation. But it was the 142 online comments that made me order a second Bloody Mary. People who knew nothing about what had happened had no qualms assuming I was a thief—or worse. *Why isn't she in jail? Why are we reading about this woman again? Art fraud? Murder? Why are you giving ink to this career criminal?* I slammed my computer shut. Damn Barbara Abrams. I vowed not to grant any more interviews.

Sonia picked me up at the airport, wearing striped bell-bottoms and a shaggy faux fur vest that on anyone with less panache would have brought to mind a gorilla. During the drive home, I poured out the whole story about Jerome and Marcel, Luc's farm, nearly getting run over, the trip to the warehouse, the shooting. I left out the part about kissing Luc. We were almost in Fairfax by the time I'd finished my saga.

"Holy crap," she finally said. "I'm glad you made it back in one piece."

"Me too."

"So you're giving up sleuthing, I hope."

"Yes," I said emphatically.

A few minutes later, Sonia dropped me off in front of my house. It was a relief to be home. Back to my garden, my dog, my long-suffering husband who put up with me. Both Jasper and

Peter greeted me with enthusiasm. Peter made a fuss over my bruises, but I assured him I was none the worse for wear.

"Something smells delicious," I said.

"I made moussaka for you. I know you love it."

OK, that settled it. If he wanted to move to Arizona, we'd make that work. He could go soon, while I concentrated on boosting business at the shop. I'd learned a thing or two from Thalia, hadn't I? Then I'd sell the business for a nice profit and join Peter. I was exceedingly grateful that I hadn't slept with Luc. I'd come close, that was for sure. Perhaps, I thought, it was guilt over Thalia's death that had pushed me toward ruining my own life. Luckily, I'd made it back from the brink.

We had dinner by candlelight, and I told Peter the whole story about the smuggling and the shooting in the warehouse. When I was finished, he pretty much said the same thing Sonia had said: time to give up playing detective. "Stop this dangerous nonsense and let the professionals handle it. Jasper and I don't want anything to happen to you."

We went upstairs to bed, leaving the dirty dishes until morning. I'd missed him, more than I'd realized. When Peter took me in his arms, I told him that I was willing to move to Arizona. "Whatever makes you happy," I said. We made love, then fell asleep with our legs entwined.

CHAPTER 32

The next day was Wednesday. The shop was closed, but thanks to my new resolve to make it a smashing success, I was there by eight, dusting and rearranging merchandise. Tilly's precious Quimper cups and saucers received a prominent place on the shelves. I was looking forward to a busy day of work tomorrow.

I tackled the mail next, sorting it into stacks. Bills to pay, receipts to file. A letter from the insurance company said the claim had been settled and the money would be in my hands within two weeks. Fabulous! I had some improvements in mind for the shop. And some of the money would help Peter get his debts paid off and even work on the rental properties. The rest would go in the bank. It felt good to know there was extra cash on hand in case of an emergency.

My contented state of mind didn't last for long, though. Thoughts of money got me pondering that blackmail note again. Who had written it? Renata, as far as I knew, had no reason to resort to extortion. Maybe Peter had been right all along. Maybe that first note hadn't been about money. What if it was just a warning to Thalia to leave Etienne alone?

Then what? I considered the possibilities. Suppose she'd told Garrett about the affair. Maybe she'd decided to leave him after all. I rejected that idea. So maybe Garrett had figured it out for himself. Thalia hadn't exactly kept her infatuation with Etienne hidden at the party. Yes, he could have figured it out. And Garrett was shrewd enough to keep the knowledge hidden. That's what made him such a good attorney.

I began pacing the store. OK, so he writes a second note to lure her to the park. He doesn't really want money, of course, but he thinks she'll show up, and he wants to get her alone. As the police said, he was close by at what's-his-name's house. He could have slipped into the park and killed her. Oh, and his gun was missing. Garrett as cold-blooded killer? Well, yes, it was possible. Especially if he knew Thalia was pregnant. That might have pushed him too far. Maybe he found a pregnancy test kit in Thalia's bathroom. Or maybe—no. Well, maybe. Maybe she told him. If she was planning to leave him for Etienne, why not tell him everything? Despite Garrett's insistence that he had no idea of the pregnancy until the autopsy, if you were capable of murder, I reasoned, you were certainly capable of lying.

Remembering how wrong I'd been about Marcel, I forced myself not to jump to conclusions. I poured a cup of coffee and sat on the deck, thinking furiously. So if Garrett had followed Thalia, and she saw him at Smitty's . . . that could have happened. And her saying "That son of a bitch" made sense because she'd think he was spying on her. She'd never connect him with the black-mail note. I made up my mind: I needed to know who Thalia saw at Smitty's. And, I decided, I also needed to talk to Fred Gibson.

"Online? Online?" a woman was shouting at the uniformed officer when I arrived at the county jail. "I can't make an appointment online. I don't have a goddamn computer. This is discrimination!"

"There are computers at the public library," the officer told her.

"I don't want to walk to the goddamn public library," the woman protested. Her weather-beaten face was framed by mousy brown hair streaked with gray. Everything about her appearance suggested she lived on the street—the gigantic backpack she carried, the tattered jeans, the filthy feet clad in frayed sandals.

"Please step over there, ma'am," the officer said to her. "What can I do for you?" he asked me.

"I have an appointment to see Fred Gibson." At this, the woman turned and gave me an appraising look. "You his lawyer?" she asked.

"No, just a friend."

"Fred ain't got friends that look like you," she said with a sneer. "What are you after, missy? Just because he's in jail don't mean that he's forgotten about me."

The officer intervened. "Ma'am," he said to her, "I'm going to have to escort you out if you continue to be disruptive."

"It's OK," I said to him. I approached the woman. "Look, I can help you make an appointment to see Fred," I offered. "We can use my phone." She grunted her assent. We sat down on two vacant chairs and made her an appointment for three the following afternoon. I offered to write down the time for her, but she was offended. "I'm not stupid," she said. "I'll be back tomorrow at three." As she tromped out, she bellowed, "I still say this is discrimination against the homeless!"

After passing through security, I was escorted into a visiting room. The place wasn't nearly the dungeon I'd expected. It looked like it was recently remodeled, with light-colored walls, plenty of windows, and new-looking, albeit uncomfortable, chairs. After a few minutes, Fred trudged in and sat on the opposite side of a glass panel, eyeing me with curiosity.

"You a lawyer?" he asked. "I already have a lawyer. Although he ain't come around in a while."

I tried explaining why I was there, but he didn't seem interested. "You got any cigarettes?" he interrupted, drumming his fingers on the faux wood tabletop.

"No. Sorry. Next time I'll bring some. What kind would you like?"

"Marlboro. Bring a case."

I made another attempt to explain why I was there. "I'm a friend of the woman you found in the park. And I don't think you killed her."

"Damn right I didn't. That's what I keep tellin' them."

"Maybe I can help you. Can we talk about the night you found her?"

"Sure. You got any chocolate?"

"Tell me about when you first saw her."

He ran his fingers through his long, stringy hair. "It's hard to remember. It's kinda hazy. But I'm sober now, you know." He smiled proudly, revealing stained, crooked teeth. "Five weeks."

"That's great! So tell me about when you found the body."

"I went to the spot where I've been camping to get into my sleeping bag. And there she was. First I thought it was my lucky day—some beautiful lady was sleeping in my spot. But I knew from the way she was lying there that she was dead. I seen plenty of dead bodies in the army.

"So then I took a look for what she had on her," he said matter-of-factly. "There was some money in her pocket and a driver's license. I took the money." He showed not a hint of embarrassment as he told me this. "Her wedding ring wouldn't come off. I woulda took that too. No use to her, is it? But I did get the bracelet. Brought it to show my girlfriend the next morning when she got off the bus from the shelter. She went crazy. Said it was real diamonds. She hid it in her underpants."

The girlfriend, who apparently was the brains of the pair, advised him not to flaunt his treasure—and not to pawn it right away. "She said if we waited for a time, no one would be looking for it. I thought a week was enough, but she said no." He shook his head sadly. "I shoulda listened to her. Then I wouldn't be locked up." After a moment, he perked up. "But it's nice and dry in here. And the food is pretty good."

"Did you take anything else?" I asked. I didn't know what kind of clue I was hoping for, but I was desperate to get some useful information.

"Nah. I kicked through all the garbage, but there wasn't nothing else worth taking."

"You didn't see a gun anywhere?"

"Shit no. I woulda grabbed that for sure. That's worth good money."

"How come you didn't take the phone?"

"What phone?"

"Her cell phone. The screen was cracked, but still . . ."

"I didn't see a phone." He shook his head. "No phone. I woulda seen it if it was there. I looked through everything."

"OK, what time did you find her?"

"About ten. Or maybe eleven. I don't really know."

"Time's up," the guard said.

Before leaving, I gave Fred the good news about the next day's visit from his girlfriend. He looked happy. "You're sure you didn't see a phone near the dead woman?" I asked one more time. He assured me he hadn't.

As I headed toward the Golden Gate Bridge, I wondered whether those guys at Smitty's had ever made contact with the mystery woman. I was convinced that whoever Thalia had seen there had some bearing on the murder. On the spur of the moment, I made a quick lane change, causing much honking, and circled back toward Fulton Street.

It took a while to find a parking spot, but I finally squeezed into one a block from the bar. The place was packed with an after-work crowd. As I expected, there were the Irish boys, playing pool. I went over to say hello.

They greeted me like an old friend. "We talked to that girl, you know," said one of them. "She was here last week. We gave her your number. Did she ever call you?"

"No." Damn. Would I ever get hold of her? "Did you tell her what I wanted?"

"Yeah. We told her you were asking about the bloke who spilled his drink on her, then dashed out. She said she hadn't seen him in here since then."

"Did she happen to say anything at all about him?"

"Nah. Just that he was a prick. But she promised she'd call you." I thanked them for their trouble and went up to the bar to buy them each a beer. When I came back to the pool table, the redhead handed me a slip of paper.

"What's this?"

"You told us to get her number, didn't you?" I kissed each of them on the cheek, then left.

CHAPTER 33

A Red Hot Chili Peppers CD was blasting as Sonia's van chugged along Sir Francis Drake Boulevard. The redwoods were thick on either side of the road, forming a verdant canopy overhead. We were on our way to pick up a vintage tiki bar and stools from a friend of a friend. Sonia had been on a hunt for just the right set for a garden design book she was working on. This one looked promising, judging from the photos the owner had sent. I'd agreed to help Sonia, albeit reluctantly. I was hoping this errand wouldn't take long.

Sonia was singing loudly as she drove. Beside her, I was lost in thought about the woman at Smitty's. Naturally, I'd phoned her as soon as I got home yesterday, only to reach her voice mail. "I won't take up more than a minute of your time," I'd promised in my message. "I just had a question about a man you met at Smitty's." Maybe she'd call, maybe not. And even if she did, I reminded myself, it could easily turn out to be a dead end. The guy who'd spilled the beer on her might have absolutely nothing to do with Thalia.

We emerged from the shade of the redwoods into the autumn sunshine of rural West Marin, where the green hills were dotted with the occasional cow. Sonia paused in her singing. "You're awfully quiet," she said. "You're thinking about the murder, aren't you?"

I didn't answer.

"I thought you were going to let that go," she said accusingly.

"I am letting it go," I protested. "That doesn't mean I can't think about it. It's not like I'm doing anything about it."

She smirked, but she didn't argue.

After a few more miles, we made a left onto Highway 1. Now that we were near the coast, the fog was rolling in. By the time we reached Bolinas it was chilly and overcast. We turned into a long gravel drive and pulled up in front of a weather-beaten farmhouse. A trim man with silver hair wearing a plaid shirt, jeans, and work boots was chopping logs in the front yard. He stopped and waved at us. "Welcome," he said as we got out of the car. "I'm Stan." We introduced ourselves. "Come on in," he invited. We followed him into the house, a fat orange cat at our heels. A fire was blazing in the living room hearth, and the smell of cinnamon wafted from the kitchen. A wiry middle-aged woman emerged from the kitchen, wiping her hands on a tea towel. "Hi, girls, I'm Gloria." She shook hands with each of us.

"I just baked some cinnamon rolls, and the kettle is on for tea," she said. We demurred, but our hosts insisted. So we sat in their knotty-pine kitchen, each of us with a plate of the buttery rolls and a mug of steaming Earl Grey tea. "I'm so glad you want the tiki bar," Gloria said. "We're going to rent the place out for two months. And nobody wants a shed full of our old stuff." She explained that they were clearing out the house and the outbuildings because they were going on an extended trip to Honduras. It turned out the couple were both marine biologists, retired now, but still avid divers. I was enjoying their company and was no longer in a hurry to get back. I reached for another cinnamon roll. They talked for a while about diving in Central America and showed us photos of their past trips.

We finished our tea, then went out to see the object of our quest. The tiki bar looked even better than in the photo. "Beautiful!" exclaimed Sonia, sliding her hand over the smooth rattan poles that formed the semicircular front. "The top needs refinishing, but that's no problem," she said. She eyed the rattan stools, which had torn aqua seats. "I have just the fabric for reupholstering these," she said. "I scored two yards of vintage bark cloth online. It will be perfect!"

As we hauled the bar out of the shed, Stan said, "We had plenty of great parties with this thing. But now it's just gathering dust. I'm glad it's going to a good home."

"Yeah, after the photo shoot, I'm definitely putting this beauty on my patio," Sonia said. The three of us loaded the furniture into the van. We thanked Stan. Gloria came out to say goodbye.

"Oh, I don't suppose you'd want a goat, too?" she asked. "Just while we're gone."

"A goat?" Sonia asked with interest.

"We've had Maisie for years," Gloria said. "She's part of the family. We'd arranged for someone to take care of her while we were gone, but the plans fell through. And the person we're renting to would rather not deal with a goat, so we're still trying to find a temporary home for her."

Of course, Sonia had to meet Maisie. And, of course, she fell in love. Even I had to admit Maisie was pretty cute as she gazed at us with her yellow goat eyes. Sonia knelt down and whispered something to Maisie while I wondered how she'd fit into the van with all that furniture.

"I'll be happy to take her," Sonia said.

"You're sure about this?" I asked.

"Oh, my other one will love her. She's very sweet." We led Maisie to the van, as Gloria went to fetch straw, food, and other supplies that she insisted on giving us.

"Don't you think we should come back for her tomorrow when we have more room?" I asked Sonia.

"There's plenty of room up front," she said. "You don't mind, do you?"

I started to protest, but Sonia was determined. "Come on, she's small."

Sonia and I lifted Maisie into the front seat, where she began pawing the upholstery. We piled in on either side of her and waved goodbye to Gloria and Stan, wishing them happy travels.

Maisie wasted no time getting comfortable. She sprawled across the front seat, her head in my lap and her hoofed legs dangling toward the floor. I hoped she would stay put for the ride home.

We were about halfway back to Fairfax when Sonia said, "Oh, damn, I was supposed to call Joe! I forgot. Do me a favor. Dial for me and put him on speaker. Now that I'm dating a cop, I don't make calls while I'm driving." I rooted around near my feet and found Sonia's purse without dislodging Maisie. I scanned through her contact list and dialed the number.

Before I could explain that it was me, Levine said, "Hello, gorgeous. I've been thinking about—"

I interrupted. "Sorry, Joe, this is Rae Sullivan. Sonia's driving, so I dialed. I'm putting you on speaker."

The two of them talked until we got to Sonia's house, joking and laughing. I marveled at how comfortable they seemed with each other. Maybe Sonia really had found the right guy.

As I absently stroked Maisie's ears, I found myself thinking of Luc's farm. And Luc. I was surprised to realize how much I missed him. Or was it the farm I was missing, the easy rhythm of a life in tune with nature's cycles? I'd only had a taste of it, but it had exerted a powerful hold on me.

Sonia said goodbye to Joe, and I put the phone back in her purse.

"I kissed Luc," I blurted out.

"What?" She turned toward me in surprise.

"Hey, watch the road."

Her head swiveled back. "What kind of kiss?"

"A good one."

She nodded, but said nothing.

"Yes. I'm not proud of myself. It just happened. I was just caught up in the moment. Paris, you know. And that farm! You should have seen him with the animals. And there were bees. And the smell. It was like Eden—"

"Yeah, yeah, I get it," she said, interrupting my homage. "I once slept with a man because of the way he talked to his dog. Turns out he was a chronic liar, but I really do understand what you're saying. And you two have the gardening connection. You know, there's a bacteria in the soil that boosts serotonin. It's an antidepressant. You two wallow in it. No wonder you like each other."

"Where did you hear about that?"

"From Joe. I told you, he knows stuff."

"Should I tell Peter?" I asked.

"About gardening?"

"No, about kissing Luc. I think I should."

"Absolutely not. It would only make him feel like crap."

"But we don't keep secrets from each other." As soon as I said it, I realized this wasn't entirely true. Peter hadn't told me about his financial troubles. But that was because he didn't want me to worry. This was sort of the same thing, wasn't it?

"There's absolutely no good that will come of telling him. It's over, right? It meant nothing. You love Peter. So there's no reason to say anything."

"I guess you're right," I said dubiously.

"Promise me! If you get some drunken urge to confess to him, you call me. I'll talk you down. Believe me, nothing good will come of telling him."

She was right. Telling Peter would make me feel better, but it would only upset him. I'd just have to live with the guilt.

When we arrived at Sonia's house, she introduced Maisie to her other goat, Lucy, then the two of us unloaded the furniture and stored it in the garage. By the time we came back out, Maisie and Lucy were munching grass together as if they'd been lifelong buddies. I headed home, taking my time driving down the hill. Some remark I'd heard during our outing was nagging at me, but I couldn't put my finger on what it was.

CHAPTER 34

Peter called up to me. "They'll be here soon, hon." Time to get ready for our guests. A few neighbors were coming over for a barbecue. True to form, the Bay Area was enjoying Indian summer, with balmy nights in October. Peter and I wanted to make the most of the weather while it lasted.

Why hadn't the woman from Smitty's called back? For reasons I couldn't articulate, I was convinced that the man who spilled his drink on her was the same person Thalia had seen when she'd said, "That son of a bitch." She'd been so focused on Marcel that she wouldn't have realized someone else was following her. A chilling thought gripped me. Luc. He needed money, according to his housekeeper. And Thalia wasn't willing to sell their property. Suppose he still bore a grudge against her for that business with his father's will. Suppose he really wasn't as fond of his half-sister as he seemed. And suppose he'd known that Thalia was pregnant. Killing her would get rid of the baby too, leaving him the sole owner of their property in Amiens. The thought of Luc as cold-blooded murderer didn't square with my memory of the gentle farmer and his beloved pigs. Still, everyone has heard about heinous acts committed by monsters with neighbors who described them as "nice."

What if Thalia told him about the first note? She might have confided in him, I reasoned. And then he had the idea to write the second blackmail note. He could have easily slipped it under her windshield wipers, since he was staying at her house. Yes, this all made sense. Then when Thalia went to leave the money, he followed her and waited in Smitty's so he could have a clear view of her getting on the bus. If she'd spotted him, she'd be annoyed, certainly. But she'd think he was there to protect her. Especially if she had told him what she was doing. In fact, I'd urged her to do just that. But wait, Luc had an alibi, didn't he? I knew the police had cleared him, so he must have accounted for his whereabouts.

"Rae, what the heck are you doing up there? They'll be here any minute." No time to think about alibis right now. I went downstairs and poured a bottle of red wine into a pitcher, then added cut-up lemons and limes, sparkling water, and fruit juice. I put the sangria in the fridge to chill. The chicken had been marinating since the night before, and the salad was made. I sliced some peaches that we'd grill for dessert. The whole time I was racking my brain, trying to recall where Luc was that night. Finally, I remembered. He'd been talking to Thalia and Garrett's neighbor in Ross at close to eight, which meant he couldn't have been in the city killing his sister. Whew.

Our friends arrived soon after, and I didn't give the murder another thought for hours. We ate too much and drank a lot of wine, while their kids ran around with Jasper. After sunset, I lit lanterns and brought out sweaters so that we could linger a while longer.

When everyone had finally gone, Peter wrapped me in his arms. "Great party," he said. I agreed. "We can clean up in the morning," he suggested.

"Good idea. I'll just bring in the plates from outside so the raccoons don't swarm." I was piling up the last of the dishes when it hit me. That phone call. When Joe Levine assumed I was Sonia. "Oh, God," I said.

"What's wrong?"

"Peter, I know how he did it."

"Who did what?"

"Peter, I think Luc killed Thalia."

He groaned. "Rae, I thought the detective shit was ending. I don't want to hear about Thalia's murder anymore."

"But, Peter—"

"No! Stop it."

"Peter, I know what happened with the phone call," I said triumphantly. "It wasn't Thalia who called me at 8:22. She was already dead. It was the murderer calling from her phone. I just assumed it was Thalia. Don't you see, the murderer must have taken her phone . . . Oh, but then he must have put it back. Because it was with her body. Hmm. Yes, he must have put it back. Peter, I really think it was Luc! I need to find out where he was that evening."

Peter was looking at me with an expression I'd never seen on his face before. I felt a chill run through my body. The phone rang, and I ran to answer it.

"Is this Rae?" asked a female voice.

"Yes."

"This is Mary Lou. From Smitty's. I hope I'm not calling too late."

"Not at all. Thanks so much for calling."

"No problem. What did you want to know?"

Peter was watching me. "Um. What did he look like? The man who spilled the drink?" I asked.

"Oh, that jerk. He was handsome. Tall and blond. About six foot two. Slim."

My throat closed. Peter's eyes were boring into me. I forced myself to sound normal. "OK, thanks very much." Covering the mouthpiece with my hand, I said, "I'll pay for the dry cleaning."

Mary Lou was still talking. "He was staring at a blonde at the bar the whole time he sat with me. And then as soon as she left, he took off like a shot. Spilled his beer all over my new sweater. At least he left money for the drinks."

"OK, thanks. Thanks very much," I said again. I hung up. "A little accident at the shop," I said in answer to Peter's questioning look. "It's all taken care of. Someone spilled something on a customer."

I felt dizzy. I had been half right. The scenario was accurate. I just had cast the wrong person as the villain. But my brain was piecing it all together now. Peter knew about the first note because I had told him! And Peter needed money. The day after the party, when Thalia got the second note, Peter had left that morning. Taking the dog for a run, he said. Oh, God. I looked up to find him watching me. The stony look in his eyes filled me with profound terror.

"I need to run out to the store, honey," I said. "I'm out of tampons." Still he stared at me. "I'll be back in a few minutes. Then we can finish cleaning up. I want to get there before they close." I grabbed my keys and the dog's leash and hurried out the front door to my car. I fumbled for a moment with the keys before getting the door open. Jasper jumped into the back seat. As I started the engine, I heard a tap on the passenger side window. I looked up to find my husband pointing a gun at my face.

CHAPTER 35

Peter motioned for me to open the car door. What if I refused? Could a bullet kill me through the window? Probably. I unlocked the doors, and Peter slid into the seat beside me. "Drive," he commanded. As he directed me through the narrow, winding streets, my mind raced. Should I crash the car? Then what? As my mind scrambled for an answer, he instructed me to park. We were just outside of Deer Park. "Let's take a little hike," Peter said. "I know how much you like hiking."

I stumbled out of the car. Jasper danced dizzily, thrilled at this nighttime outing. "Let's go," Peter said. I could feel the gun at my back. How did Peter have a gun? We started walking into the park. We had no flashlight. I thought furiously. If I could make a run for it, he might not be able to find me in the dark. But Jasper would bound right after me, I knew, making it impossible to hide.

We stumbled along, a small sliver of moonlight making the ground just barely visible. After several minutes of walking, the trail started to rise. I slowed my pace, but he poked the gun into my back again and said, "Keep going." Maybe the gun had no bullets, I prayed. Was it the gun he had killed Thalia with? How many times had he fired it? How many bullets did a gun hold, anyway? I wondered. I tried to reason with him. "Peter, you know I love you. Can't we go home and talk about this?"

"Keep walking," he said.

I started to cry. "Peter, please."

"Shut up." I thought of Luc as I walked along sobbing. He'd never tell me to shut up. I hoped he'd speak at my funeral. I tried to imagine what he might say. I looked at the stars high above the peak of Mount Tamalpais. My last night on earth. At least I was in a place I loved.

"I know that you wanted me to do it," Peter said. He sounded absolutely deranged. I suspected that it was pointless to argue with him. But at least he was talking. Maybe he'd change his mind about killing me.

"That's why you told me about the note," Peter said knowingly. "You told me Thalia was being blackmailed and that she'd pay. You told me, Rae. I knew you wanted me to do it. I always did know what you wanted, sometimes even before you did." Then his voice became angry. "That bitch. She set me up. She didn't leave the money!"

"So you killed her for the insurance money?" I wailed. "How could you?"

"What?" He laughed contemptuously. "No, of course not. I didn't even know about the insurance money. That was a nice little surprise. You know what she said when she saw me in the park? She said, 'I'm calling Rae. What were you doing with that girl at Smitty's?' That girl was *nothing*. I only sat with her because Thalia walked in. She was supposed to get on the goddamn bus! She was supposed to leave the fucking money! But no, she had to screw it all up.

"I couldn't let her call you, could I? I grabbed her phone. I think that's when she realized why I was really there. For the money, of course. I needed the money. *We* needed it. Do you have any idea how much money I owed? And the people I owed it to were not very nice people, Rae. They even threatened to come after you, to hurt you. We needed that money! That's when she pulled out a goddamn gun. She was going to shoot me!"

So Thalia had gone to the park armed. I could have told her that wasn't going to end well. "Peter, that makes it self-defense," I said, seizing on something that might bring him to his senses. "That means it's not your fault. You don't have to—"

"She had to die," Peter said matter-of-factly. "Because what was to stop her from telling you? I couldn't have that, could I?

"I took off my raincoat and wrapped it around the gun. It barely made a sound when I shot her. And the phone. Well, that was clever, wasn't it? I phoned you from the awards dinner because you said you were going to call the police. I wanted you to think Thalia was calling. Of course, I had to put the phone back. I drove by after the dinner. The body was still there in the bushes. It was so easy—the perfect murder," he gloated. "Except you couldn't let it go, could you? Even when the police arrested someone. You had to keep—"

Hearing the rustling of an animal in the bushes, Jasper began to whine. "Shut up," Peter said sharply as we continued on, the path quite steep and twisty now.

"That bitch was going to turn you against me." His voice took on a note of hysteria. "Like she always tried to do. She was jealous of us."

"Peter, I'd never turn against you. You know I love you," I lied.

"Bullshit. If I gave you the chance you'd run so fast, and you'd take me down with you."

I continued to sob as I stumbled along. Jasper tugged at his leash, oblivious to the danger. What would happen to Jasper after I was gone? Maybe Sonia would take him. Yes, I consoled myself. Sonia would take him. She wouldn't let Jasper live with this monster.

We were coming to a steeper part now, with lots of switchbacks. I knew this area. I'd once crashed my bike on this very turn. Maybe Peter would stumble. If he did, could I get the gun from him? Probably not. The canopy of trees overhead was thick now, making it difficult to see. Suppose I jumped off the side, slid down the mountain. Then what? With a broken leg—or worse—I couldn't get far. It was many, many hours until morning. He'd find me before then, before any hikers or dog walkers came along. My phone rang. I reached into my pocket.

"Let it ring," Peter commanded.

I wanted to answer it and shout, "Help! My husband is going to kill me!" But I let it ring. After four rings, it stopped. A moment later it rang again.

"Shut the damn thing off. Now."

I slipped the ringing phone out of my pocket to comply. I recognized the number. It was Detective Hernandez. What would happen if I answered it and screamed? Probably get shot in the back.

"Shut it off," Peter said in a steely voice. I stood frozen, looking at the phone in my hand. My last link to help. Peter snatched it from me and tossed it toward the trees. It sailed off over the side of the path. The drop was so far that I didn't hear it land. I wanted to keep him talking, buying me time. Maybe we'd run into someone, anyone, out for a moonlight hike.

Jasper stopped and poked his nose into a clump of ferns, whimpering with excitement. Then he gave a low, deep growl. "Shut up," Peter said, and he kicked him. The dog let out a yelp. Without even thinking about it, I turned around and shoved

Peter hard with both hands in the center of his chest, catching him by surprise. He stumbled, cursing, then slipped over the side of the trail, the sound of breaking branches mingling with his screams. I took off like a shot, running faster than I could have imagined, Jasper bounding at my heels. I didn't stop until we reached my car. Gasping, I tried to pull open the door. It was locked. I felt in my pockets for the keys, then saw them lying in a heap on the floor of the front seat, where the contents of my purse had spilled out.

"Come on, boy," I said, taking hold of the dog's leash. I was too winded to run now, but I covered the ten blocks to my house at a near trot, looking over my shoulder every few minutes. Even though Peter was presumably lying at the bottom of a hill, I couldn't shake the feeling that he was going to show up behind me brandishing that gun.

To my surprise, there were two Fairfax police cars in front of the house, lights flashing. I stumbled up the front stairs and opened the door. A uniformed police officer confronted me. "Are you Rae Sullivan, ma'am?"

When I nodded, he immediately got on his radio. "She's here. We've got her."

There was a crackling response that I couldn't make out. "No, just her," the officer said. More crackling. "Yeah, she's OK."

Zombie-like, I walked to the kitchen to make sure Jasper had water. There was Sonia, standing at a sink full of soapy water, washing dishes. When Jasper ran to his bowl and started slurping, Sonia turned and saw me. "You're home!" she shrieked. "Oh, thank God." She embraced me with fervor, soapy water running off her yellow rubber gloves. "Thank God. Thank God. They're out searching for you."

"What . . . What . . . How did you know . . . ?"

"Hernandez knew," Sonia was saying. "He knew it was Peter, but he thought you were still in France. He was planning to make an arrest in the next day or two. But then when Joe Levine found out you were already back, he told Hernandez, who realized you were in danger."

"Excuse me." One of the uniformed officers was standing in the kitchen. "Mrs. Sullivan, we need to take a statement. And Detective Hernandez is on his way," the officer told me. "He was very happy to hear that you're safe."

Sonia peeled off the gloves and threw them on the kitchen counter. "Come, let's go sit." We went into the living room, and I sank onto the couch. It felt sublime to sit down. I recounted the harrowing events of the evening, with Sonia holding my hand.

When I was finished, the officer said, "Now about your husband. We need to locate him as soon as possible. Can you tell me where you last saw him?"

I shuddered as I remembered Peter's icy voice and the gun at my back. "He's on the trail. In Deer Park. Well, he's off the trail, actually." I tried to describe where exactly Peter might be, but the officer was clearly not a hiker—or, if he was, he'd never been on this particular trail. My landmarks of low-hanging manzanita and large boulders meant nothing to him. He tried to pin me down on mileage, but I had no idea.

Finally, Hernandez arrived. He conferred briefly with the officer, then sat down next to me. "I'm very glad you're safe," he said.

I nodded. "My husband probably needs help. I . . . I pushed him off the trail." I could swear Hernandez was trying not to smile. "Please. Go get him." For the second time, I tried to explain exactly where Peter was. I could hear a helicopter circling overhead. This was more drama than my quiet little neighborhood had ever seen.

Hernandez went and conferred with two other policemen, then came back to the couch. "Mrs. Sullivan, it would be very helpful if you could lead us to the spot."

"No," I said without hesitation. I couldn't go back. I was tired, so tired, and Peter had a gun. And my thigh muscles ached from running. I leaned back into the soft couch cushions and closed my eyes.

"Mrs. Sullivan," Hernandez said gently, "I wouldn't ask you to do this unless I thought it necessary. You'll be completely safe, I assure you. One officer will stay here with your friend and the other will come with us."

"It's OK," Sonia said. "You go. I'll stay here with Jasper. When you come back I'll make you a stiff drink."

"OK." I got up wearily. Hernandez and one other officer drove to the trailhead, following my directions. Hernandez did a lot of talking on his radio—something about dogs and helicopters. "You were right, you know," I said to Hernandez. "About the fraud at the gallery." He pursed his lips but said nothing. "I knew—or at least suspected—something wasn't right. But I kept quiet."

Hernandez nodded. "That's not important now," he said. "What matters is that you're safe and that we're going to arrest your husband." I felt an enormous relief at confessing to Hernandez, trivial as my sin was in the scheme of things. Maybe this was why people went to church, to admit their failings without being judged. We parked the car, not far from my Volvo, and got out, taking powerful flashlights from the trunk.

"This way," I said. The moon was high now. We crossed the meadow. I inhaled the smell of eucalyptus. Mount Tam rose before me majestically. With the two men at my side, we started up the trail.

CHAPTER 36

The shop was bustling. If Thalia's murder had been good for business, my attempted murder was even better. I'd hired three new part-timers, who were all terrific. And the funny thing was, I liked being in charge. I'd thought I couldn't do it without Thalia, but in a way things were easier.

Peter's trial had been an ordeal. The fact that I had told him about Renata's note to Thalia was twisted by the defense into an act of betrayal on my part. They tried to paint me as somehow complicit in Thalia's death. Well, perhaps it *was* partially my fault. Perhaps I had set this all in motion. I'd have to live with that. Now that six months had passed, it didn't hurt quite as much, although I still missed Thalia daily.

Peter was sentenced to twenty years in prison. Of course, I thought he should get life, but since Thalia had been the one with the gun, his lawyer successfully made a case for self-defense. Trying to kill me later was what got him the twenty years.

The *Chronicle* had reported every sordid detail of the lengthy trial. Barbara Abrams covered the story. Although I refused to grant her any interviews, she pieced together a flattering portrait of me as naive victim. "I never thought you were guilty," she admitted in an email. "Sorry I dredged up all that past shit, but it's what readers wanted."

And she redeemed herself further when she phoned me one morning in November. "You're going to love this!" she rasped in her gravelly smoker's voice. "I've been revisiting that art fraud story ever since I met you. I did a hell of a lot of digging. My exposé is running tomorrow. You have to check it out. Turns out Hubert Grebe was in on it with that bitch boss of yours, Virginia! They're arresting his ass in Santa Fe. Just goes to show, you can't trust anyone, can you?"

Indeed.

"I'm going to take off a little early today," I told my new assistant.

"No problem, boss. I've got it under control."

I stopped at the grocery store and tied Jasper up out front, where he received multiple pats on the head and probably illicit snacks. Then we drove home to our new little cottage on Porteous Street, just blocks from our old house. I'd had no trouble renting out the Hickory Street house. It was, after all, beautiful. Apparently, having been occupied by a murderous lunatic only added to its cachet. And I was willing to rent to pet owners, which made it a hot property. I used the insurance money from Thalia's death to buy the tiny cottage, which suited me perfectly. It had only one bedroom, but it was flooded with sunlight and had an overgrown backyard that I'd begun to tame.

The feeling of coming home to my very own house was delicious. The framed picture of Thalia and me stood on my bedside table. I looked at it often, marveling at how young we were, how certain we'd been that we had our whole lives ahead of us.

I put the groceries away and started dinner preparations. Sonia and Joe were coming over. Not only were they still dating; they were even toying with the idea of getting married.

My sucrine lettuce was thriving in the new raised beds I'd built. I talked to Luc every few weeks, but I hadn't seen him since our escapade. This summer, if my employees were seasoned enough, maybe I'd sneak away for a week. If not, that was OK. I knew he and the "girls" would be waiting for me whenever I decided to visit.

ACKNOWLEDGMENTS

This book was a long time coming to fruition. It's all too easy to let a full-time job, a family, and life in general get in the way of writing. My profound gratitude to those who encouraged me to stick with it, convincing me I had an entertaining story worth telling: Julia McNeal, Julie McCullough, Donna Mettier, Debbie Clay, Maggi Garloff, Kate Fitzsimmons, Alice Watkins, and Mary Lou King.

For their guidance and astute comments, heartfelt thanks to Leslie Keenan, Wendy Tokunaga, and David Corbett. Thank you also to Catherine Hunter for her brilliant copyediting and to Barrett Briske for her eagle-eyed proofreading. A shout-out to She Writes Press for its unflagging support of authors. Ditto to Book Passage, one of the great indie bookstores and a devoted friend of writers. For help spreading the word, I'm indebted to Crystal Patriarche and Savannah Harrelson, my enthusiastic publicists at BookSparks, and to Marcia Norris. And special thanks to Dan Monte, who never let my bedtime conversations about murder alarm him.

ABOUT THE AUTHOR

Bonnie Monte, originally from Brooklyn, lives in northern California with her husband, dog, and turtle. When not working as an editor and copywriter, she likes to hike, garden, and—of course—read mysteries.

SELECTED TITLES FROM SHE WRITES PRESS

She Writes Press is an independent publishing company founded to serve women writers everywhere. Visit us at www.shewritespress.com.

The Tolling of Mercedes Bell by Jennifer Dwight. $18.95, 978-1-63152-070-9. When she meets a magnetic lawyer at her work, recently widowed Mercedes Bell unwittingly drinks a noxious cocktail of grief, legal intrigue, desire, and deception—but when she realizes that her life and her daughter's safety hang in the balance, she is jolted into action.

Water On the Moon by Jean P. Moore. $16.95, 978-1-938314-61-2. When her home is destroyed in a freak accident, Lidia Raven, a divorced mother of two, is plunged into a mystery that involves her entire family.

Last Seen by J. L. Doucette. $16.95, 978-1-63152-202-4. When a traumatized reporter goes missing in the Wyoming wilderness, the therapist who knows her secrets is drawn into the investigation—and she comes face-to-face with terrifying answers regarding her own difficult past.

Watchdogs by Patricia Watts. $16.95, 978-1-938314-34-6. When journalist Julia Wilkes returns to the town where her career got its start, she is forced to face some old ghosts—and some new enemies.

Murder Under The Bridge: A Palestine Mystery by Kate Raphael. $16.95, 978-1-63152-960-3. Rania, a Palestinian police detective with a young son, meets cheeky Jewish-American feminist Chloe at an Israeli checkpoint—and soon becomes embroiled in a murder case that implicates the highest echelons of the Israeli military.

Glass Shatters by Michelle Meyers. $16.95, 978-1-63152-018-1. Following the mysterious disappearance of his wife and daughter, scientist Charles Lang goes to desperate lengths to escape his past and reinvent himself.